THE TWELFTH URBAN FARM FRESH ROMANCE

Together in Thyme

VALERIE COMER

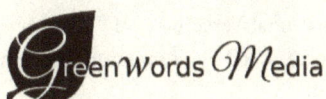
GreenWords Media

ACKNOWLEDGMENTS

Thank you for being a faithful reader of the Urban Farm Fresh Romance series! You've stuck around for twelve novels, and I appreciate you so much.

Thanks to Elizabeth Maddrey, first reader, idea-bouncer and excellent author in your own right. Thank you for providing sanity, humor, and kicks in the pants as needed!

Thanks to my reader group on Facebook, who chipped in on the research to remind me what had already been written about Hailey North in the previous Urban Farm Fresh Romance novels. I appreciate all of you very much: Cindi, Anke, Paula, Amy, Jenelle, Connie, Lisa, Monique, Samantha, Carrie Ann, and Melynda. Thank you bunches!

A big thank you to my fabulous editor, Nicole, who sees beyond words, punctuation, and sentence structure to the heart of the story.

I'm also grateful for the Christian Indie Authors Facebook group and my sister bloggers at Inspy Romance. These folks make a difference in my life every single day. I'm thrilled to walk beside them as we tell stories for Jesus!

Thank you to my Facebook friends, followers, street team, and reader group members for prayers, encouragement, and great fellowship.

Thanks to my husband, Jim, for research trips to Spokane (although not during this coronavirus pandemic which has closed the Canada/USA border!) and talking through scenarios as needed — to say nothing of everyday love and support — and to my kids and grandkids for cheering me on and embracing the idiosyncrasies of having an author for a mom and grandmother.

All my love and gratitude goes to Jesus, the One who invited me to experience His unending and passionate love and walks beside me every day. My prayer is that you see His love anew through the pages of this story.

Bibliography of Valerie Comer's Books

Complete List of Titles by Series and Original Release Month
*Denotes title was in a multi-author box set. Scroll down for details!

Urban Farm Fresh Romance
(complete in 2021)

0. Promise of Peppermint (March 2017)
1. Secrets of Sunbeams* (July 2016)
2. Butterflies on Breezes (August 2016)
3. Memories of Mist (July 2017)
4. Wishes on Wildflowers (February 2018)
5. Flavors of Forever (September 2018)
6. Raindrops on Radishes (February 2019)
7. Dancing at Daybreak (September 2019)
8. Glimpses of Gossamer (February 2020)
9. Lavished with Lavender (June 2020)
10. Cadence of Cranberries (December 2020)
11. Joys of Juniper (April 2021)
12. Together in Thyme (November 2021)

Pot of Gold Geocaching Romance
(complete in 2021)

1. Topaz Treasure* (May 2021)
2. Ruby Radiance* (September 2021)
3. Sapphire Sentiments (July 2021)
4. Amethyst Attraction (August 2021)

Christmas Romance at the Miss Snowflake Pageant
(complete in 2017)

1. More Than a Tiara* (September 2014)
2. Other Than a Halo (November 2016)
3. Better Than a Crown (September 2017)

Farm Fresh Romance
(complete in 2016)

1. Raspberries and Vinegar* (July 2013)
2. Wild Mint Tea* (March 2014)
3. Sweetened with Honey (November 2014)
4. Dandelions for Dinner (March 2015)
5. Plum Upside Down (August 2015)
6. Berry on Top (February 2016)

Cavanagh Cowboys Romance
(Montana Ranches Christian Romance, ongoing)

1. Marry Me for Real, Cowboy (September 2020)
2. Give Me Another Chance, Cowboy (February 2021)
3. Let Me Off Easy, Cowboy (September 2021)

Saddle Springs Romance
(Montana Ranches Christian Romance, complete in 2020)

1. The Cowboy's Christmas Reunion* (October 2018)
2. The Cowboy's Mixed-Up Matchmaker (Dec 2018)
3. The Cowboy's Romantic Dreamer (April 2019)
4. The Cowboy's Convenient Marriage (June 2019)
5. The Cowboy's Belated Discovery (November 2019)
6. The Cowboy's Reluctant Bride (April 2020)

Garden Grown Romance
(Arcadia Valley Romance, complete in 2018)

1. Sown in Love* (January 2017)
2. Sprouts of Love (May 2017)
3. Rooted in Love (November 2017)
4. Harvest of Love (May 2018)

Riverbend Romance Novellas
(complete in 2015)

1. Secretly Yours (February 2015)
2. Pinky Promise (April 2015)
3. Sweet Serenade* (July 2015)
4. Team Bride (October 2015)
5. Merry Kisses* (November 2015)

http://valeriecomer.com/books

*H*e was back in town.

Hailey North hated that her heart sped up at the sight of him walking into her bistro. She'd been doing just fine without Basil Santoro in her life, thank you very much. He'd left Bridgeview in disgrace three years back, which added up to over one thousand days she'd waffled over whether she wished he'd return or stay away forever.

Fickle heart.

She should detest him. She mostly did.

He might've entered her café, but there was no way she was fixing the guy a coffee or even talking to him. Not if she could help it. "Astrid! You're needed over here."

The middle-aged server glanced over. "Coming right up." She patted a woman's shoulder as she topped off her coffee cup.

Basil shifted closer to the counter. "What, you don't know how to use your own fancy coffee machine?" Amusement glinted in his blue eyes.

"I run the kitchen. Kass runs the floor." Only, her

cousin's toddler had thrown up all night, and Kass had begged off. They usually had enough staff to cover, but Bridgeview Bakery and Bistro had been extra busy all morning, and Hailey had been called out of the kitchen more than once.

"Good morning! What can I get you?" Astrid turned to Basil.

Hailey turned away to avoid his lingering gaze. She could answer the question for him, unless working at the Fireweed Restaurant in Seattle had fancied him up. For Basil, it had always been...

"Just coffee. Black."

And he hadn't changed. He was likely incapable of it. Something she needed to keep in the forefront of her mind.

"Do you have a few minutes, Hailey? You look like you could use a break."

She stilled in the doorway to the kitchen. Such flattery, telling a woman she looked tired. "Sorry. Too much to do." Too many regrets to block from her mind.

Astrid smiled brightly. "It's your usual time for a break. There's a bit of a lull, and Julissa comes in in five minutes."

Thanks, Astrid. "I'd rather n—"

"Afraid of me, Hailey? Tsk."

She pivoted back and gave Basil a hard glare. "Afraid of you? Not in your wildest dreams."

His eyebrows bobbed as a grin creased his face. "Oh, I wouldn't want to tell you about my wildest dreams. Or... maybe I should?"

Hailey stiffened. If she could throw the man out into the busy street on his backside, she'd do it in a heartbeat. After everything he'd done. Things no one else knew, but he sure did. Not that he knew quite everything, and she wasn't about to enlighten him.

This was her place of business. Hers and her cousin Kassidy's. She couldn't yell and scream and demand he leave the premises, but it would certainly feel therapeutic.

Not that he'd listen. That sardonic grin was his trademark. The only time she'd seen it disappear was when he'd been sentenced to jail after his drunk-driving conviction three years ago. The facade had shifted then. He'd done his time then moved to Seattle, but it didn't look like he'd changed at the core.

Rumor had it he'd quit drinking, not that Hailey paid attention to gossip. Okay, she totally did, especially if Basil's name came up. And if the source was his sister, Jasmine, one of Hailey's closest friends. That pair of siblings had never gotten along as kids — or as adults — and Jasmine had been furious with Basil over the DUI.

Hailey shoved all that out of her head.

Astrid rang up Basil's coffee.

He raised his eyebrows at Hailey. "Come on, Hailey. I don't bite."

Since when?

Basil smirked.

"A hazelnut latte, Hailey?" Astrid glanced between them. "I can fix it with monk-fruit sweetener and even go decaf if you prefer."

"Sugar-free. Impressive." Basil took a sip from his mug, his gaze still fixed on Hailey.

"We try to flex with the times." Hailey stared him down. "We do a brisk business with folks trying to cut sugar out of their diet."

"Please don't tell me you've tampered with your cinnamon roll recipe."

"Never."

Astrid coughed.

Hailey sighed. "We did introduce a keto version as well, but it's not nearly as popular." Astrid had poked and harassed Hailey and Kass to expand into that market, and it had been worth it. Now Astrid acted like she was part-owner instead of part-time staff.

Basil pulled his wallet back out. "Well, now you have me curious. I'd like to try the keto version."

Hailey narrowed her gaze at him. "It's on the house." Why on earth had she said that?

His eyebrows shot up.

Maybe she'd done it to shock him, and it had worked. She picked up the tongs, set a roll on a small plate, and handed it across the turquoise bakery case. "I'll be interested in your thoughts."

No, she wouldn't be.

"I'm happy to pay..." He studied her face. "Never mind. Thank you."

The espresso machine hissed, but Hailey didn't break her gaze from Basil's. It might be childish, like whoever looked away first was the loser. Or she might just be filling her memory banks with his blue eyes, his wavy dark hair, and the scruff on his chin.

"Join me?" he invited again, quieter.

"Here's your hazelnut latte, Hailey." Astrid set it on the counter. "Decaf and sugar-free, just what you need."

Now she'd look like a petulant child by refusing, but she'd speak to Astrid later about usurping authority. "Fine. I can take five minutes."

"Julissa can finish up lunch prep when she comes in," Astrid said.

That woman. If she wasn't Kass's husband's ex-mother-in-law, she'd be fired. That *ex* should count for something.

"Preference where we sit?" Basil poked his chin toward the corner table.

Hailey was going to regret this big time. She already did... except for the part of her that thrilled to his nearness.

She wouldn't think twice about sitting down with any of their other male clients, including Basil's brothers or cousins, though she'd only flirt with the singles. She had standards.

But Basil? He'd always been in a category of his own. Like playing with fire.

She'd already been burned.

BASIL SANTORO WOULD TOTALLY HAVE GONE for the fist pump if he didn't have a plate in one hand and a mug in the other. Of course, the action would have backfired. Hailey would hightail it back into the bistro's kitchen like a hurricane-force wind, but seeing her angry was kind of a win on its own.

Yeah, yeah. Not a particularly mature thought and, at thirty-three, he should be well on his way to adulthood. Wasn't that everyone's comment to him all the time? *Grow up, Basil.* This time he heard it in his sister Jasmine's voice.

He settled into the bright yellow chair in the corner and glanced toward the counter. Yep, this spot still had a perfect view straight into the depths of the kitchen. It wasn't fair to make Hailey sit with her back to her customers, but whatever. He'd be here long after she stormed off in anger, frustration, or both.

Basil broke off a piece of the cinnamon roll and glanced at Hailey.

She'd only improved with age, much like a fine wine. Right, he wasn't thinking about alcohol these days. She must be thirty now — she was his sister's age, and Jasmine had turned the big three-oh in spring. Hailey tugged her blond, chin-length hair out of its net and fluffed it with her fingers.

Vain, his Hailey.

Only... not his.

"Looks like you guys keep busy. You've been open, what, six years now?"

She nodded. Sipped her latte.

What must it be like to have a vision for one's future, buckle in through thick and thin, and make a go of it?

Basil had drifted. He'd tried the college route but dropped out and slid from one job to the next. His older brother had helped him get a job with City of Spokane Public Works. He'd done everything from shoveling sidewalks to fixing manhole covers to watering flower boxes. Whee. Talk about fulfilling.

"You afraid of a keto cinnamon roll?" Hailey eyed the pastry still in his hand.

"Should I be?" He quirked an eyebrow at her as he popped the bite into his mouth. The temptation to dramatize gagging then holler for water flared, but he withstood. "Not bad. The texture isn't as melt-in-your-mouth as the originals, though."

Hailey visibly relaxed. "Almond flour just doesn't react the same as wheat."

Huh. She actually cared about his opinion? "No, it doesn't."

She looked at him, eyebrows raised. "You've been experimenting?"

"You have no idea what I've been doing the past few years."

"Serving at a restaurant in Seattle."

Basil grinned. "The most elite restaurant. Tips were amazing." Not so amazing he hadn't taken on other jobs on the side, though.

"Well, that's nice for you, I'm sure. Thanks for gracing my humble establishment, which is nowhere near as fancy as what you're accustomed to."

Ooh, those blue eyes shot daggers at him. This was more the Hailey he knew and loved. No. Not loved. He'd burned any potential bridges a long time ago. "This place has plenty of hometown charm."

"Just call it quaint and be done with it."

"Okay. Quaint."

"Some things never change." She gritted her teeth.

"You told me to say that." He leaned across the table and looked her in the eye. "I always do what you tell me."

Red flashed up her cheeks, and she surged to her feet. "You're insufferable."

"As you say." For a second, he thought she'd dump the remains of her mug in his lap, but she swept away. Behind the counter, she emptied the latte down the drain then set the cup in the bin. She stuffed her hair into its net while retreating to the kitchen.

"What's with Hailey?"

Basil looked up to see his cousin Peter setting his briefcase on the vacated chair. He shrugged. "You know how she gets in these moods."

Peter frowned thoughtfully. "I'm going to grab a coffee. Be right back. Hey, is that one of the keto cinnamon rolls? My wife loves those things."

"Yeah. Not bad."

"Not bad? Hailey's a genius."

Thankfully, Peter didn't wait for a reply but headed for the counter. The short, older woman — Astrid, Hailey had called her — rang up his order then Peter returned and removed a sheaf of papers from his briefcase.

"Are you absolutely certain you want to do this?" Taking his seat, Peter studied Basil.

Time for that grownup bit to kick in. "Absolutely. I've been socking away as much as possible for three years. I'm ready to buy back in."

"A lot has changed. Your sister and I have worked our fingers to the bone to get Bridgeview Backyards to where it is now. We're farming sixteen backyards and have dozens of subscribers to the organic box program. And we're always scrambling for seasonal workers. Jason and Landon both graduated from high school in May and are headed away for college soon. We can't count on them coming back next summer... and we still have a brutally busy wrap-up in the next couple of months."

"How does Jasmine manage with a toddler?"

Peter looked at him as though Basil should know the answer already. "Lillian is in daycare in the mornings, and then Nathan keeps her for the afternoon. Thankfully, he works from home and can manage his clients while Lillian naps."

Jasmine was nothing if not dedicated. Basil had to hand

it to her. She would have been the perfect firstborn but had landed in the middle with two brothers on either side. She'd always hated that Basil was older.

Astrid set Peter's coffee down and topped off Basil's without asking if he wanted more. When she moved on to the next table, Peter slid the papers across. "Here's our updated business plan and financial statements. I want you to take your time and read through all of it before committing."

Did he need to sound like he thought Basil would ditch them again? Like Basil had enjoyed leaving the company in a lurch three years ago! No one wanted to be hauled through court and force his partners to buy him out to pay his fines. Yeah, he'd pretended it was no big deal. What else was he supposed to do? Apologize? Grovel? That wasn't his style.

Maybe it was time for a different approach.

Movement in the kitchen caught Basil's eye. Hailey leaned over her worktable, rolling out pastry. She looked strong. In control.

Gorgeous.

Wasn't stupidity doing the same thing over and over but hoping for different results?

Actually changing meant admitting he'd been wrong all these years. That he'd been selfish. Arrogant. Everyone who knew him already knew all that.

But changing meant letting his guard down. Letting people see who he was on the inside. They wouldn't like him any better with the added insight.

Especially not Hailey.

2

*T*he problem with having never told anyone about her teenage fling with Basil meant Hailey couldn't dump her current turmoil on any of her friends.

She paced her apartment above the bistro, the place still feeling empty, though Kass had married Wesley and moved out nearly three years before.

Everyone got married. Kass. Eden. Jasmine. Everyone Hailey had ever considered a friend, but not her. Not ever. She'd flirt like she didn't care and save her heartache for private moments. With the bistro well established and Kass long gone, the quiet times were far too many.

The memories of that summer in Italy were also far too many.

Basil was back.

Hailey pivoted on her heel and marched down the short hallway, swung around, and came back.

Why couldn't he have just stayed away? He'd worked at the Fireweed. Hailey hadn't been to Seattle in years, but she'd heard of the Fireweed even before Basil joined their staff. It made Bridgeview Bakery and Bistro seem like a kid's lemonade stand.

Peter had passed papers to Basil. They'd sat and talked long enough that Astrid had refilled their coffee twice. They'd walked out together, clapping each other on the shoulder, the sheaf tucked under Basil's arm.

What was in them? She was dying to know.

Peter and Jasmine owned Bridgeview Backyards. Basil had once been a co-owner. Was he looking for work with his cousin and sister?

They were constantly seeking out steady employees, but those were usually high school or college kids needing summer jobs. Basil didn't fit that category.

That stack of papers had been thick. Really thick. No potential employee needed that much info.

Hailey glanced at the clock then reached for her phone before she thought better of it. Tapped Jasmine's number.

"Hi, Hailey! Just a sec."

She heard muffled deep voices then Jasmine came back more clearly. "I just handed Lillian over to Nathan and Basil. Now I'm out on the deck where it's quieter. What's up?"

Hailey managed a chuckle. "Do I need a reason to call my best friend?"

"Probably not. Can you believe Lillian adores her uncle Basil? Who'd have guessed?"

"He thinks he has a way with females, so maybe it's not surprising it starts with toddlers."

Jasmine giggled. "So true."

Hailey took a deep breath. "I saw he was in town. Is he staying with you and Nathan?"

"Believe it or not, he rented an apartment in

Bridgeview Manor. He bummed some furniture from Marley's house, since she moved in with Alex after the wedding."

Who cared about Alex and Marley right now? "Oh, wow. He must be planning to stay, then."

"So he says. He met with Peter, and he's buying back into the business. I just hope he doesn't flake out on us again."

Hailey gulped. It seemed two parts of her life were crashing together. She'd never have signed her own agreement with Jasmine and Peter if she'd had even a niggle of worry that Basil might return. They'd offered a deal to overhaul her building's flat rooftop and turn it into a combination garden and eating area, similar to the one on Antonio's Italian Restaurant just down the block. They'd care for the vegetables, and Hailey and Kass would get a cut on the bistro's veggie bill.

She forced her attention back to the conversation. "Buying back in? I'm surprised. I thought he really enjoyed living in Seattle."

He'd made such a big deal of escaping the confines of the few blocks where most of the Santoro clan live.

Hailey could only look on enviously from the outside. She and Kass were both only children with no other cousins, even on the other sides of their families. Kass's parents lived in northern Idaho, but Hailey's were diplomats currently stationed in the Middle East. They'd moved so often and in such dangerous circles that Hailey had spent much of her childhood and teen years with her grandparents in Spokane. Even they were gone now, but they'd left the old brick building to her and Kass.

This was her entire legacy. Compared to Basil's rich

heritage with four generations and a dozen or more cousins living nearby, it wasn't much.

With a start, she realized Jasmine was still talking about the funds her brother had saved up to reinvest in Bridgeview Backyards. "And he's done some carpentry work, too. I know he'll be an asset to getting our upcoming infrastructure projects underway. In fact, you'll be glad to know he'll be able to have a look at your rooftop next week and probably get started right away."

Oh. Yeah. Hailey'd be totally glad of that. Not. "I, uh... it's okay. The original timeline for later in the fall is fine by me."

Jasmine laughed. "We need projects to ease Basil back into things before the guys go off to college, and yours is perfect."

No way was she explaining to Jasmine just why hers *wasn't* perfect. Not after all these years. That summer was water long passed beneath the bridge, just like the glimpses she had of the Spokane River between the buildings across the street, flowing swiftly toward the Pacific Ocean.

"Whatever works for you, I guess." Hailey faked a yawn, but it turned into a real one. "I should get to bed. Four o'clock comes mighty early."

"I don't know how you do it."

"I'm used to it after six years. I roll out of bed at three-thirty. Thankfully, it's a short commute."

Jasmine laughed. "I'd kill myself tripping down those steep stairs half-asleep. Take care, Hailey. Thanks for calling. It seems I hardly see you anymore."

"I know, right? Talk to you soon."

Hailey ended the call and headed to the kitchen for a

ginger ale. She stopped before opening the fridge. Did she really need a sugar rush right before bed?

Drat Astrid anyway. Life had been so much simpler before she'd vilified sugar in Hailey's life.

Fine. A glass of water then.

∽

BASIL SCRUNCHED his nose at the curly-haired toddler snuggled in her daddy's lap, and the tot fluttered her eyelashes back at him.

Too bad Hailey had perfected the glare for him and saved the eyelashes for every other man on the planet.

Nathan chuckled. "She's usually shy with strangers."

"I'm hurt. I'm no stranger, and she knows that."

"Well, you haven't been around much in her life. Plus, she's got a short memory."

Whereas Hailey's rivaled an elephant's. What were she and Jasmine talking about, anyway? Jasmine's laugh came through the glass door from the deck, but he couldn't make out any words.

"We should get you to babysit one evening. I haven't taken my wife out on a real date in far too long."

Right. Basil was nothing if not available. Still, after that DUI three years ago, he should simply be thankful if his brother-in-law trusted him with his daughter.

Odds of ever marrying and having kids of his own were slim to none, so he might as well soak up his niece and nephews. Rough-housing with Marco's boys was less daunting than this fragile female child.

Lillian watched him from her safe spot.

"Yeah, I could probably do that. Not so fond of diapers,

though." He'd avoided caring for his nephews at that stage.

Nathan shrugged. "They're not that bad. She usually poops in the morning, anyway."

"Ugh. Do I have to know her personal potty habits?"

"I do, as well." Nathan grinned. "How about you?"

Basil clamped his hands over his ears. "La la la."

His brother-in-law let out a guffaw, startling Lillian, who pushed her pudgy hands against his chest. "Dada."

Oh, man. What a sweet little voice. Basil was a goner.

The patio door slid on its rollers, and Jasmine came back inside, setting her phone on the table. She looked between them. "What are you guys staring at me for? Come to Mama, Lillian. It's bedtime."

The toddler burrowed deeper in her daddy's arms. "Dada."

Nathan surged to his feet. "I've got her. Gonna teach your big brother about diapers so he can watch her Friday night. You don't have plans Friday, do you, Basil?" Without waiting for an answer, he continued, "because you, Mrs. Hamelin, are going on a date with your husband."

Jasmine raised one eyebrow as she crossed her arms over her chest. "A date sounds nice, but we could try Gabriella or Simone."

Basil pressed his hand to his heart. "You wound me. I'd love to look after your little princess."

"Then come with me." Nathan beckoned. "Basil's got it, love."

Basil followed his brother-in-law into the nursery. No unicorns or rainbows here, thank goodness. Lots of green with pink accents, including a ginormous tree with pink blossoms painted around a corner of the room. "Who's the artist?"

"Daria and Fran took over. Looks good, huh? Jas likes it." Nathan laid his wiggly daughter on a padded surface.

"They did a good job, for sure." Daria was his brother Marco's wife, while Francesca was one of their cousins.

Basil figured he should pay attention to his niece's care. A few minutes later, the little one was tucked in footy pajamas and held her arms out to him. He snuggled her against his chest.

How had he stayed away from Bridgeview this long? Yeah, it had taken a while to save up enough to come home with his head held high, but he'd missed so much in the meanwhile.

Hadn't that kind of been the point, though? To break the bonds with the Santoro clan? He couldn't handle the disapproving scowl his nonna always wore in his presence. The way the aunts tsked and the uncles shook their heads. The way his siblings and cousins pretended he wasn't there or that he had nothing worthwhile to add.

He'd done that to himself. Played on it. Faked liking it.

No more. The new Basil was rock solid. He'd never touch alcohol again, let alone drive under its influence. He was an upstanding citizen, worthy of the respect of his relatives and neighbors. Certainly responsible enough to babysit a toddler.

Whether Hailey would ever speak to him willingly or not was up for debate. And then there was—

"Coming to church on Sunday?"

And then there was that. God had let Basil down a few too many times. He couldn't trust Him. But he also couldn't avoid Bridgeview Bible Church if he wanted his family to see him as stable and mature.

"Of course. Wouldn't miss it for anything."

3

*K*ass turned to Hailey after church. "Want to come for lunch? Seems forever since we've caught up on things."

"We see each other every day."

"Like two coworkers. Not like cousins or friends." Kass laughed. "So, unless you have other plans firmed up, please come."

Being around her cousin's family fed a restlessness inside Hailey, a reminder that Kass had everything Hailey wanted. Not Wesley. Not his eight-year-old son, Sebastian, either, though the kid was pretty all right. Not even their toddler, Eleanor. It was the complete package: an adoring husband, a family, a home filled with love and laughter.

What Kass had was a life outside of work. Hailey merely existed in her off-hours. Ouch.

Kass nudged Hailey's elbow. "Don't overthink it. Just say yes."

What else was she going to do on a hot summer afternoon? Sit inside the apartment and play an online game? "Okay. I'm not sure how long I can stay—"

At *the look*, Hailey zipped it and gathered her purse and Bible. "Can I bring something?" The least she could do was be gracious.

"Just you."

Basil laughed.

Hailey froze then turned just enough to see him from the corner of her eye. Lucky for him, he seemed to be talking to Peter and Sadie, so the laughter wasn't at Hailey's expense. Besides, it wouldn't be fair of him to mock her for being single, since he was in the same boat.

Did Kass know Basil would be representing Bridgeview Backyards on the rooftop project? Maybe Hailey wouldn't need to tell her today, since they had a no-shop-talk policy on weekends unless by special meeting.

"I'll swing by the apartment and get changed into something more comfortable," she told Kass.

"Great. Don't be long, though. Lunch is already prepped in the fridge, and Eleanor needs her nap soon."

Hailey edged past a few more of their friends and made her way toward the foyer, saying hello to everyone. She loved Bridgeview Bible Church. It had been her spiritual home since she'd been a kid.

Adriana Sheridan stretched toward her. "Hailey! Want to come for lunch? Myles and I are having a few friends over."

"Not today, but thank you. I'm going over to Kass and Wesley's."

"Oh, too bad! We'll catch you another time."

And here Hailey'd thought she could get away with a solo day. But that gave her far too much time to think, anyway. Since there was a line to shake Pastor Tomas's hand, she slid out the open doors and started down the steps.

"What a crush in there."

Hailey stumbled on the step and would have tripped if Basil hadn't caught her arm. She wrenched free. "You startled me."

He chuckled, a low rumbling sound. "Sorry. I have that effect on people. I heard you turn Adriana down. She invited me, too, and I was hoping you'd come."

Since when? "Nope."

"But we can walk over together, anyway, since your cousin lives next door."

"I'm stopping at home to change." Of course, Basil wouldn't need to. He was prepared for anything already in nice shorts and a short-sleeved untucked shirt.

He gave her a once-over. "You look great."

A flush shot up her cheeks. "Thank you." She'd never admit she'd thought of Basil when choosing this teal sundress this morning with its flirty layered skirt, wondering if he'd notice. If he'd like what he saw.

Thoughts she had no business dredging up, not after all these years. He shouldn't be in her head at all. Ever.

They'd reached the edge of the parking lot by now, and he seemed determined to walk beside her. Both his hands were pushed into his pockets. And she was supposed to think of casual conversation? She caught sight of Antonio's down the block. "I'm surprised you didn't go to work for Tony."

Basil's eyebrows quirked. "Work for my cousin? Are you kidding me?"

"Why would I be? You served at Fireweed. You said you

made good money. Your cousin has won some awards for his Italian restaurant."

"Good for him."

What was that supposed to mean? "You're jealous of him?"

"I have no clue where you'd get that kind of idea from." He scowled. "You, of all people, should realize some of us want to control our own destinies, not merely support someone else's."

"Our grandparents left Kass and me the building and all the contents. I'm not sure we controlled anything."

"Sure, you did. You could have sold the whole shebang and had working capital to start any business you wanted, anywhere."

"True. That never crossed our minds."

"But you chose your destiny."

"I guess." Why was she arguing with Basil over something so stupid? Because opposing him was an ingrained, natural response. Last time she'd agreed with him... no. She wasn't diving into her pool of memories. Not now. Not ever.

Hailey shook the thoughts away. "You've done a lousy job of choosing your own destiny."

"Make one mistake, and no one ever forgets."

She spun to face him, hands on her hips. "One mistake? Seriously?"

He shrugged. "Okay, a couple of them."

"You could have killed someone." And she had. She stalked down the sidewalk as quickly as she could in her stupid heels. Running shoes would have been better suited to her mood, but then, she didn't own any. She never ran.

Except from the truth.

"But I didn't." Basil was still beside her.

Hailey sped up, but he only shifted from sauntering to walking. "Leave me alone."

"Hailey."

"What?" She glanced at him, caught her stiletto in a crack on the sidewalk, and pitched. Or she would have, if he hadn't caught her.

Basil grinned. "Every time you fall for me, you make this far easier than it ought to be."

Hailey shoved his hands off and marched away. "Don't touch me."

"You'd rather have hit the cement?" He resumed pace beside her again.

"Yes."

He laughed, shaking his head. "Oh, Hailey. I'm not that bad. We once had a good thing going."

"That was *not* a good thing."

"Seeing Venice together in a gondola?"

"That part was fine." She sent him a full-on glare and turned to punch in the lock-code at the back of the bakery. "Don't bother waiting. I'll be a while."

Hailey slid through the door and yanked it shut, thankful for the automatic lock. She leaned against the metal door for a moment, willing Basil to go away. Maybe she'd take ten minutes then let herself out the front door instead. Anything to create some distance from Basil Santoro.

THERE WAS no point in trying to deal with Hailey when she got like this. Basil shrugged and strode down the street toward the Sheridans' house a few blocks away. They lived in a sweeping contemporary at the bend of the river, which had always seemed well-suited to Adriana's style of entertaining. That woman loved to cook. Her new husband, Myles — well, probably he wasn't new anymore. They'd been married for just a few months before Basil's DUI.

Hailey was right. He might not have been in an accident that night, but that didn't mean it hadn't been stupid. Flirting with Dixie had been the first dumb thing that day. Just because she and Dan had been fighting didn't mean she'd been free for pick-up, no matter how she acted. Taking her to the bar had been the second stupid thing. And then driving drunk and attempting to run the police blockade had been the icing on the cake.

Yeah, he'd deserved arrest. He'd paid his fines, done his jail time, and survived without his driver's license for twenty-four long months. He'd discharged his debt to society.

Maybe he hadn't paid his debt to Dixie and Dan. Was there really any way to do that? They seemed solid together now, and reminding them might only stir up old hurts.

Hailey sure prickled at bringing up the past. He'd always looked at those two weeks in Venice as an idyllic interlude in his otherwise stifled life. He'd gone to Italy for the summer to reconnect with his extended family and taken the time to do some sightseeing. Running into his little sister's best friend at the Basilica di San Marco had been serendipitous. Hailey North had been abroad to visit her diplomat parents, who'd been stationed in Rome at the time, but she had the entire summer free.

They'd toured Venice together. The Grand Canal. Torcello Island. Countless palaces and cathedrals and museums, They'd dined at the best hole-in-the-wall cafés and drank perhaps a little too much wine.

They'd done a few other things together, too.

He'd kind of thought they'd pick up where they left off when they returned to Bridgeview that September. With a little more decorum, of course. His older brother had married young — why couldn't Basil do the same?

Oh, maybe because Hailey refused to acknowledge his existence when they met again at home. It was like Venice had never existed.

Well, fine. He could prove it didn't matter to him, either. If that's how she wanted to play the game, he'd one-up her. His flirting and don't-care attitude were superior to hers. Just watch.

All that had gotten him absolutely nowhere for twelve stupid years. Nowhere but regrets and a woman who refused to walk down the sidewalk beside him for three blocks to her cousin's house. Okay. He wasn't dense. He'd have to come up with a real plan to discuss Italy and whatever hang-up she had about that summer.

Basil headed toward Myles and Adriana's without looking back to see if Hailey followed. Better yet, he veered onto the riverfront pathway at Wade and Rebekah's place and pretended he cared about the shade of the cottonwoods and whether the redbands were rising. He hadn't fished in a long time, but no one knew or cared.

Wasn't that just a snapshot of his life? No one cared.

It wasn't true. His parents cared. His siblings cared, even though they didn't trust him not to screw up again. Nonna cared, possibly too much. She probably prayed for his repentance five times a day and ten on Sundays.

Wouldn't they all be surprised to find out he'd been doing some deep thinking lately?

Why couldn't he have that conversation with anyone? How about Marco? No. His perfect older brother wouldn't understand. Nor would Alex, and Evan was nothing but a kid even though he was in his final year of law school. Basil certainly wasn't dumping his life on Jasmine. His cousin Peter, maybe. They'd been close once.

He shook his head as he made his way through Sheridans' carport and into the huge backyard that sloped toward the river. Garden beds overflowed with vibrant flowers and leafy vegetables, and chickens darted around the entire yard while a small gray cat napped on the roof of their coop. From the trees at the far end, Basil heard kids' voices. There must be a treehouse up in there somewhere.

Adult voices came from the deck, and he turned toward them.

"Hey, Basil! Thanks for coming." Myles Sheridan brandished a pair of grilling tongs in his direction. "We're glad to see you've returned to Bridgeview."

Basil managed his trademark easy grin. "How can a guy stay away?" Though he'd surely been tempted.

Logan Dermott came down the deck steps and clapped Basil on the shoulder. "Good to see you."

"Hey there." Basil smacked him in return then looked up as the French doors swung open.

Dixie came out carrying a large, covered bowl. "Basil," she said warily.

"Here, let me get that." Basil bounded up the steps, but she'd already set her load on the long table by the door. "Uh, is there more inside that needs to come out? I can help."

She gave him a measuring look. "Can you?"

Ouch. "Of course." He really should figure out how to make amends.

At that moment, Dixie's husband, Dan, came through the patio doors. He grinned at Basil, which was nervous-making right there. If anyone had good reason to pound Basil into the ground, it was Dan Ranta. He might not have been married to Dixie when Basil had made his move, but Dixie had given birth to Dan's son not that long before.

What were you thinking? He could hear the accusation in Dad's voice. In Uncle Al's — *may he rest in peace* — and all his brothers'. And in Jasmine's snippy tone, of course.

The thing was, he'd made a career out of not thinking. Of not caring. Of rocking the boat and laughing when anyone admonished him.

Basil took a deep breath and looked between Dixie and Dan. There was no time like the present. "I just want the both of you to know I'm really sorry about everything that happened that summer."

Dan slid his arm around Dixie's waist and tugged her against him. Then his gaze probed Basil. "You know, I wanted to keep holding a grudge — trust me — but I can't do it. Not in the light of how much God has forgiven me for."

"Uh. Thanks." Dan's words weren't quite an acceptance, were they?

"I was stupid, too, but Dan's right." Dixie looked up at her husband, her face softening with love. "I'm also sorry for so much. Dan's forgiven me. God's forgiven me. I hope you will, too."

"Yes. Of course." Maybe Basil could move on from it now.

"But the most important thing is clearing it up with God," Dan went on. "If you haven't confessed your sin to Him, that's gotta be your next step, because all the rest doesn't really matter."

"Your forgiveness matters to me."

"But God's is worth far more."

"You might be right."

Dan studied Basil, not giving an inch. "You know it's true. You were brought up with the truth. I sure wasn't. I'm thankful for my sister and Logan sharing God's love with me, but you already know how this all works."

"Knowing and doing are two different things," Basil said quietly.

"Then it's time to put it into practice."

4

*H*ailey untied her apron as she glanced over at Julissa. "Everything okay if I head out now?"

The prep cook nodded as she focused on assembling a sandwich with the bakery's fragrant sourdough bread. "We've got it, just like we always do."

After this many years working with Reina and Julissa, Hailey should know. But it still seemed strange to abdicate her kitchen to employees for so many hours while the bistro remained open.

"You'll start the—"

"Sourdough. You know I will."

"Okay. I'll be upstairs if you need anything."

Reina pulled cookies out of the oven. "We know. Go on with you, now."

Hailey's nerves didn't usually get to her this much. It might have to do with Basil having spent coffee hour in the bistro with his dad and uncles. It might have to do with their appointment in an hour up on the rooftop. Kass was taking a bit of time off — she worked the floor from ten to cleanup — and they'd see what Bridgeview Backyards had planned for their garden.

Hailey had tried to back out of the rooftop plan on Sunday afternoon, but her cousin had latched onto the idea with the strength of an industrial magnet. Unless the sketches or estimates were way out of the ballpark, this project would move ahead.

And that would mean Hailey would find it difficult to avoid Basil during construction.

She helped herself to a container of gazpacho from the walk-in cooler and headed up the back stairs. Once in her apartment, she popped open a ginger ale — take *that*, Astrid — and settled at the kitchen table with her laptop open.

An email from Mom. Well, that was unusual. Hailey clicked to open it.

Hello, Darling,

We've got a few weeks of leave this fall and thought we'd come by Spokane. I'm sure you have a spare room for your parents, right? It seems ages since we've seen you.

Love, Mother

It seemed ages, because it had been. Her parents had always expected Hailey to come to them, at least after Grandma and Grandpa passed on. But since she and Kass had reopened the bakery and bistro, she hadn't been free to gallivant the globe. That meant she hadn't joined them for their vacations in New Zealand or Peru or Greece for the past six years.

They finally missed her enough to come to her. Yeah, she wasn't going to take that too personally.

Hailey ate a few more bites of the chilled soup then pushed it away. So much for her appetite. Her gut had already been twisting because of this afternoon's meeting, and now this.

A rap sounded at the door. "Hails?" came Kass's voice.

Hailey unlocked the door. "Hi. My parents are coming to visit."

"When?" Her cousin stepped inside. Kass knew better than to think it was good news. She knew their history.

Hailey sighed. "September."

"I'm sure it will be fine. Right?"

"One can hope," Hailey muttered.

"Are we meeting Basil here or on the roof?"

"On the roof." Not a chance was she inviting him into her personal space. She glanced at the clock. "We could go up already. He won't be long." Unless he blew them off.

"You've got time to finish your lunch."

"I'm not that hungry."

"Hailey, you need to eat. Did you stop for a break all morning?"

"I had a cinnamon roll."

"That's not real food, and you know it."

"Astrid is rubbing off on you."

Kass laughed. "As if. Sit down, cuz, and eat your soup."

"Do I *have* to, Mom?" Hailey put her best whine into her voice.

"Yes, you do. Go ahead. I'll grab something to drink from the fridge while I wait."

"All I have is ginger ale."

"It'll do."

"Aren't you afraid Astrid will find out?" Hailey took a bite of soup.

A can hissed, and Kass came back into the main room.

"If you tattle, I'll tell on you. I think our secret is safe right here, don't you?"

Aw, man, Hailey missed living with Kass. Not that she resented Wesley and Sebastian and Eleanor in Kass's life; she just hated being left behind.

Kass dropped into the other chair and pointed her pop can toward Hailey's bowl. "Eat."

"I am, I am," Hailey grumbled. But she ate the last few bites, and it did settle her tummy a little. "I wonder why they're coming now."

"They miss you."

"So they say." Absurd thought. They'd never missed her before. Hailey surged to her feet. "Let's go up to the roof."

"Sure. I still think this is genius." Kass hurried over to the door. "I was jealous when Tony built his rooftop patio. I don't know why I assumed we couldn't do the same."

"Maybe we can't. Maybe Basil will find a structural problem. Maybe he doesn't even know what he's talking about." That was the most likely.

"Didn't Peter send over a structural engineer a couple of weeks ago? The report looked fine."

"Oh. That. I forgot."

Kass raised her eyebrows then swept up the final flight of stairs ahead of Hailey. "I'm glad we're adding an outside staircase instead of using this one for the public."

"It's too steep. Too narrow."

"I know." Kass emerged onto the graveled surface. "Ugh. I'll be glad when there's a railing."

"Me, too. It's a great view, though." Hailey headed to the side overlooking the street and river. "I guess this will be where the tables go."

Behind her, the door creaked open again. She didn't turn.

"Hey, Basil!" greeted Kass. "I'm so happy for you to be back at Bridgeview Backyards."

"It's good to be home. Hi, Hailey."

She couldn't keep her back to him and retain any semblance of civility, so she turned. "Hi."

Their eyes locked for a few seconds, and Hailey felt the electric charge pass between them as it always did. Then Basil swept the hand holding a clipboard. "This is great. Peter gave me the dimensions and the location of the new stairwell, so I took the liberty of drawing up some preliminary plans."

Oh, look at him being all mature and responsible and everything.

Kass reached for the clipboard. "Let's see. I'm so excited."

That made one of them. Hailey had been thrilled a week or two ago. Now, not so much.

"So, the stairs will come up over here." Basil walked over to the east edge. "Peter said that's what you'd agreed on, right?"

"We don't have any other options, other than revamping the inside stairs," Kass replied. "Being on the street corner eliminates two sides, and there isn't room in the back alley. We haven't really done anything with that sliver of land on the east side, though." She peered over the edge.

Hailey knew what she saw. They ran a weed-eater through the patch between their building and the one next door a few times every summer. Thankfully none of the bistro windows faced that direction.

"What do you think, Hailey?" Basil turned toward her.

Guess she needed to get over herself and participate in the conversation.

⁓

"I THOUGHT you said Hailey was the driving force behind the project." Not for the first time, Basil wished a glass of wine or a can of beer were a viable option. A can of pop lacked a certain something.

Jasmine dropped into a chair across from him and around the corner from Peter. "She is."

"Kass asked all the questions. Hailey held back like she didn't even care." And Basil had repeatedly tried to engage her that afternoon, but she'd been resistant to the end.

Peter scowled. "That's weird."

Jasmine narrowed her eyes at Basil. "I think I know exactly when she stopped caring."

He raised his brows. "Oh?"

"She began backpedaling when I told her you'd be on the project."

The old Basil would have snapped out some egotistical response like how Hailey couldn't stand to be in the presence of greatness. The new Basil managed to keep it zipped.

"Since when does Hailey have a problem with Basil?" Peter looked between them.

Since the twenty-third of June, twelve years ago. Not that Basil was about to share.

"I've always wondered about the two of you..." began Jasmine.

Basil shook his head. "Nothing to wonder about."

Peter leaned forward on his elbows. "But if you are Hailey's problem with the project—"

"If you need to take me off it, I'll understand."

"Are you *sure* you don't know why?" probed Jasmine.

"If I knew, why would I tell my nosy little sister?"

"Because it affects your nosy little sister's livelihood as well as your own."

"Look, I'll pick tomatoes and melons and eggplant and whatever all you've got growing. *You* work with Hailey."

Jasmine shook her head. "It took me half an hour to sketch my ideas for that rooftop then Peter laughed and said my proportions were totally off. So, I'm pretty sure I don't have a future in construction design."

Maybe Basil didn't, either. At least not atop the old brick bakery.

Crossing his arms, Peter leaned back in his chair. "You flirt all the time. Hailey flirts all the time. Seems to me you two would be a match made in heaven."

"That's the old me." Basil managed to keep his gaze focused on his cousin. "We might have once had a little spark, but it's long gone."

"I knew it!" Jasmine's eyes glinted.

Man, he should have kept his mouth shut. "It's not like you think." It had been far, far more than his kid sister could possibly guess. Unless Hailey had divulged their story upon her return to Bridgeview that fall. Was that why Jasmine had no respect for her big brother? No. He'd managed that all on his own. If Jasmine knew his history with Hailey, she'd have confronted him straight up.

"What was it like then? And when?"

"Give it up, Jas. It's not relevant." Basil tapped the sketches he'd been working on.

"It's totally relevant if Hailey doesn't want to work with you."

"Nah, she'll be fine. I shouldn't have said anything. The important thing is the design. I stole some ideas from Tony's rooftop. He managed to get quite a few vegetable beds in there while making a great dining atmosphere."

Jasmine gave him a long look.

Peter pulled the papers toward himself and shuffled between them. "Biggest difference is that Antonio's patio is only open in the evening, where the bistro is open over lunch. Ah, good. Lots of shade covering."

"We used this style of retractable awning at the Fireweed. I ran some numbers. It's not that much more costly than a bunch of individual umbrellas, and it will last much longer."

"And gives better coverage." Peter nodded. "I like it."

"Not too much shade for the vegetables?" Jasmine dragged the top paper over.

"It will be filtered light, but there'll still be plenty of it."

"I like this bit." Peter pointed at the design. "Putting a kitchen staging area and a dumbwaiter on the south side is perfect. It keeps the inside stairs more private plus blocks the ugly alley view."

"Staff parking. The dumpster." Jasmine nodded. "I hate to say it, bro, but this is a good design."

Basil could finally drag in a full breath. Since when did he care so much what his little sister thought of him? "Only good? I thought you could call it great. Or awesome. You could even mention I'm a genius."

She rolled her eyes. "I could also mention you have a big head, but I figured that was an established fact that didn't need repeating every single day for the rest of our lives."

"Aw, tell me how you really feel."

Jasmine got up, rounded the table, and slammed a punch into his shoulder.

"Ow! What was that for?" He rubbed the spot.

"That's just a preface for what I'm going to do next."

He winced away. "Now I'm terrified."

She messed up his hair with both her hands. "I love you, stupid. Don't let it go to your head."

Peter grunted. "You two. Can we get serious here? Do we have cost estimates in place? A contractor for the staircase?"

"A friend of Uncle Dino's can fit it in. Best of all, he recently demoed a brick building over by the interstate and offered the salvaged brick."

Jasmine took her seat again. "Similar shades as the building? Even better. I'm sure Hailey's happy."

Basil wasn't going for that bait. "I haven't told her and Kass yet. I just found out this morning. There are still a few more quotes to come in before I've got a complete picture to share."

"Looks good." Peter stacked up the papers and set them in front of Basil. "Told you he'd do a good job, Jas."

Figured it would be Peter who'd give Basil another chance, but that he could talk Jasmine into it? Totally amazing.

"I won't let you guys down."

Jasmine stared at him hard. "You'd better not."

5

*D*idn't you just put salt in that?"

Her scoop hovering over the container of pink Himalayan salt, Hailey froze at the sound of Reina's voice. "I did?" Had she been about to double up on this poor recipe she'd made thousands of times?

"I think so."

Great. Reina didn't sound certain. Did any alternative exist besides pitching the contents of her mixing bowl and starting over? But it was still weeks before they'd get a new shipment from the farm co-op growing their grain. She didn't dare waste any.

Never mind setting her morning back by half an hour. Hailey measured half the amount onto the dough and set the giant mixer's blades rotating. The bread might be a little too salty — or not quite salty enough — but it wouldn't be a tossup of all or nothing.

They had too many pickup orders for that afternoon to start over. Running a CSB, or community supported bakery, along with a bustling bistro meant Hailey and her kitchen staff kept to a pretty tight schedule. Some days she blessed the layer of stability the standing orders provided for their business. Today it felt more like a curse.

It was only 4:30 am, and she was already eight minutes behind. That would never do.

"I've got the muffins going," Reina announced from the other side of the worktable. "Since it's the church group this morning."

Hailey nodded. They opened early for the men's prayer breakfast on Thursdays, which meant Reina's schedule shifted a half hour earlier. Hailey's first priority had to be getting all the bread and buns rising or they wouldn't be ready for lunch. But the cinnamon rolls needed preparing, too. Julissa had left the dough in the walk-in like she did every day.

Hailey tossed it onto her worktable. Maybe she should hire another kitchen worker, even part-time. Or perhaps one worker could serve a dual purpose, a few hours on the bistro side and a few hours prepping? She'd have to ask Kass if one of the front staff needed more hours.

The back door opened. "Hello in there!" called Basil.

Was this how it would be with him working on the roof? He had no reason to be in her kitchen. She glanced over her shoulder. "Yes? What do you need?"

His hand pressed over his heart. "No, 'good morning'? No 'nice to see you'? Nothing?"

"Good morning. What do you need?" Because Hailey didn't have time for games. Especially not with him.

"Good morning to you, too. Just letting you know we'll have a crew up and down your back stairs all day, since that's currently the only way to access the rooftop."

"Okay." Thankfully, Kass, with her penchant for sleeping in, no longer lived up there.

"Okay, then."

Basil was still in her space? She glanced over. "Anything else?"

"Dino and Zeke will be delivering several pallets of bricks later this morning. I told them they could come in the alley. Do you have any other place you can park your car for a few weeks?"

"Are you serious? This is where I live."

"It's also a construction zone, and we need a spot to stash building materials. Zeke has begun erecting a fence around the area to keep snoops and thieves out."

Hailey sighed. "Sure. Whatever. When do you need it moved?"

"By about ten o'clock?"

She'd just toss her keys at him and make him do the deed if they weren't upstairs in her apartment. "Could I have a little more advance notice in the future?"

"Sorry about that. Zeke had a free day because of the rain, so he shifted gears."

The weather was a concern for the grain farm, she knew that. Maybe she could blame her grumpy mood on the gray skies. But, no. She'd been off-kilter since Basil strolled back into her life like he had a right to be there. Oh, and since her parents had decided to show up. "Fine. I'll take five as soon as I can and move the car. Anything else?"

His gaze dropped to her work surface. "Are you making cinnamon rolls?"

Hailey stifled a smart-aleck response. "Yes."

"Will they be ready for men's prayer breakfast?"

Her eyebrows shot up. Since when did Basil attend that?

He sure hadn't when he lived in Bridgeview before. "No. We've got savory egg muffins and—" She glanced at Reina.

"Cherry," Reina supplied.

"And cherry pistachio muffins for the group. The bistro doesn't actually open until seven."

"I'll get one on my way out then. Or later, since I'll be nearby all day." He flashed her a flirty grin. "All day, every day for a few weeks."

That didn't even bear discussing. Hailey turned back to the mound of dough, cut off a segment, and attacked it with her rolling pin.

"I love to see a woman in the kitchen."

She stilled, but her temper flared. "Get out."

He chuckled softly. "I'm leaving."

"Good." She didn't take another breath until she heard the door click. When she glanced over, the spot he'd been standing was mercifully empty.

"He's a brash one, isn't he?" remarked Reina, sounding all too casual.

"He is."

"One of those Santoros."

Whatever she meant by that. Hailey nodded.

Reina sighed. "Such good-looking men with their black hair and blue eyes."

Hailey glanced at her worker sharply. Reina was fifty if she was a day and married to boot.

"What, I can look and appreciate, can't I?"

There was no appropriate response. Hailey pivoted for the softened butter to spread on the dough. Drat. She'd forgotten to take it out of the walk-in. Basil was messing with her head in more ways than one.

While Hailey sorted out the butter, Reina set the other

mixer churning with the muffin batter. One of the wall ovens beeped, announcing its arrival at the set temperature. Reina would start on the egg muffins next, but Hailey needed to stay on track for the baked goods that would grace the display cases upon opening, as well as today's CSB pickups. Chewy chocolate peppermint cookies would be next, once the cinnamon rolls were all rising.

She had no room in her head for Basil Santoro.

⌐—ᴇ·ᴄ

"GOOD TO SEE YOU, BASIL." Myles Sheridan nodded at him as other guys from the neighborhood gathered around the set of pulled-together tables.

Basil managed a grin. "You, too." This was a new experience. The church guys had met like this long before his DUI, but he'd never deigned to join them. At first, he'd made excuses. He worked too early. He had other responsibilities. He'd overslept his alarm. Eventually they'd stopped asking, which had been the goal.

Being in church most Sundays — well, half of them, give or take — was all the religion he'd been able to stomach, especially since his relatives wouldn't stop talking about God like He was one of the family.

Funny how some time in lockup then three years away gave a guy a different perspective. He'd been the dude who didn't care who he stomped on on the way up, because he wasn't coming back down.

And now he was eating crow, mostly of his own free will. If a man could call it free will when God kept showing up in his life, forcing him to face the mess he'd made.

The older woman Basil had seen in the kitchen carried

in a tray of coffee cups and set it on a nearby table. "Help yourself!"

"Thanks, Reina," Jacob Riehl said. "Hey, where's Hailey this morning?"

The woman shot such a quick glance at Basil he almost didn't notice. "Busy in the kitchen. She asked me to serve today."

By which Basil assumed this was usually Hailey's thing. Had he set her behind with his brief poke into the kitchen? More likely, she was simply avoiding him. Normally he'd count it a win if he disrupted someone's life, especially hers. Now he'd rather catch another glimpse of her than agitate her. Huh.

He picked up a coffee and took a seat part way down one long side.

His brother Alex dropped into a chair beside him. "Hey."

"Hey, yourself." Basil glanced at Alex's mug. "You drink your coffee black, too?"

Alex grinned. "Dad would have it no other way."

True. All that 'drink it like a man' and 'it'll put hair on your chest' stuff from their childhood.

"At least it's not strong enough to stand a spoon up in like Nonna prefers hers."

Basil had never bothered with a stovetop espresso machine like Nonna's moka pressure pot. Yeah, he'd enjoyed the thick, fresh brew that summer in Italy, but preparing it was too much hassle for everyday use. Unless you were Nonna.

"Who's got something to share?" Jacob looked around the table. "Anyone?"

"I do." Logan leaned forward. "You guys know we want

to start a family, but it's just not been happening. TMI. Sorry." He shot a glance at Basil. "But I've been reading in Isaiah lately, and 49:8 really spoke to me. Mind if I read it?"

Some of the men murmured acquiescence.

"Goes like this." Logan cleared his throat and looked down at his phone. "'Yahweh says: "When the time of showing you favor has come, I will answer your heart's cry. I will help you in the day of salvation, for I have fixed my eyes on you. I have made you a covenant people to restore the land and to settle families on forgotten inheritances."'"

He looked around. "I know there's a context present that has nothing to do with Linnea and me, but it was just a great reminder that God's timing is perfect. He's still watching over us, and when the time of showing favor arrives, He'll answer our hearts' cry. I think that's amazing."

Basil eyed the men. All of them were married, except for him. Most of them had families. Lots of them were younger than him, including his kid brother. Hadn't this group started with a bunch of young bucks seeking their place in the world? And now they were worried about when God would answer their prayers for children.

He shifted slightly in his chair. He might be in the wrong place, but there wasn't really a better one.

"There's a lot in the Bible about things happening at the right time," Myles Sheridan said. "I'm thinking of Psalm 69:13: 'but I keep calling out to you, Yahweh! I know you will bend down to listen to me, for now is the season of favor. Because of your faithful love for me, your answer to my prayer will be my sure salvation.'"

"That represents a whole lot of faith," put in Peter.

"In every circumstance," agreed Jacob. "It's part of

recognizing God's sovereignty, I think. We know He hasn't forgotten us and that He has our best interests at heart."

All that sounded great, but how about the guy who'd literally walked away from God? Because these verses seemed to talk about people who wanted God's will. Basil might now, sort of, but how did he know he'd be welcomed back? And he barely remembered how.

"Sorry it took so long." Reina set down a couple of platters on the table behind Basil. "I'll go get a fresh pot of coffee for you guys, too."

"Who wants to pray?" asked Jacob.

Alex flashed his hand then ducked his head. "Lord, thank You for this group of guys, and thank You my brother's here today. Also thank You for this great breakfast, and I ask Your blessing on Hailey and Reina for taking such good care of us. In Jesus' name, amen."

"Amen." Chairs scraped as men rose to help themselves to the fragrant sweet and savory muffins.

But Alex was still seated. Basil raised his eyebrows at his brother. "Thankful for me being here, huh?"

"Yeah, I am." Alex met his gaze full on.

"Uh, cool. It's not so bad. And the breakfast smells good." Basil broke contact and surged to his feet. He didn't belong here. He'd be too busy to come again next week. It wouldn't even be a stretch, since construction would have started on the outdoor staircase, and Zeke preferred to start at dawn then shut down operations before the full heat of the day.

Curiosity had gotten the better of Basil this morning, but it wouldn't happen again. This wasn't his crowd.

"Here, want some?" Dan Ranta extended a plate toward Basil.

"Thanks." This wasn't Dan's scene, either. Or at least, it hadn't been — the guy's drinking had been on par with Basil's in the old days. But Dan and Dixie had dove right into the whole Jesus thing with a baptism and a wedding all the same day. Now they took their three kids to church every Sunday.

Maybe Dan was the kind of guy Basil could talk to. That is, if he ever wanted to share his deepest thoughts with anyone.

Nah. Totally unlikely. He'd dip into this sphere just enough to fit in, but that radical deep-end stuff? That was fine for guys like Dan who really needed it.

Basil would keep his balance on the tight-wire of life.

6

O h, I'm so glad you came over!" Adriana gushed as she poured two coffees. "It seems I hardly ever see you."

Guilt poked at Hailey. Five days in the bakery and a day of church and friend stuff generally had her craving a bit of downtime on Mondays.

She accepted the coffee, perched on a tall stool at the island, and looked around at Adriana's magazine-worthy kitchen. "Where's Jamie?"

"He's decided he's too big for naps, but he gets so cranky. Myles took him to the park. Hopefully he'll fall asleep right after dinner. The two-year-old, not his dad."

Hailey grinned. "I figured."

"So, what have you been up to? I'm honored you gave me a call today."

"I had to get out of my place. The workers have been clomping up and down the stairs to access the roof since dawn."

"Ugh." Adriana scrunched her face. "I thought they were building an outside access?"

"Two different work crews, so that's in progress as well."

"It will be gorgeous when it's finished." Adriana set a plate of cookies on the island and settled on the other stool.

"It will. I can hardly wait." What Hailey *really* couldn't wait for was Basil to go away. Knowing he was likely making some of that noise forced her out of the building. What if she ran into him outside her door? Awkward.

"Will you get to use it yet this season?"

Hailey blinked. Use what? Oh, the rooftop garden. "Jasmine says they can plant some fall crops up there. Spinach, peas — that sort of thing. And they'll plant some flowers."

"Edible ones like nasturtiums?"

"Probably. I buy them for our salads, anyway."

"It will be such a nice spot to eat lunch or enjoy a coffee with friends."

"I hope so. I'm not sure if I'll get the chance to use it much myself, but it will be nice for others."

Adriana laughed. "You can entertain when the bistro is closed. Dining up there overlooking the river on Sunday evenings with a group of friends? Count me in. We'll do a potluck the first time to see how the space works."

"That sounds like a great idea. Kass and I used to have friends over." When all their girlfriends were single. No one their age was solo anymore except Hailey, and she wasn't about to start hanging out with the twenty-year-old college girls.

"Lots changed for you when she married Wesley." Adriana took a sip, not looking at Hailey.

"Yes." It hadn't been a question. "But it's good to see her so happy and settled. She's always wanted a family."

"I love having her and Wesley next door, though we rarely see each other since she works long hours."

If that was supposed to induce guilt, it missed the mark. Reopening their grandparents' bakery was a dream Hailey and Kass had shared equally. They both worked more than full-time, but that came with owning a bustling business. It wasn't Hailey's fault Kass was married with two kids while she herself was single.

"Basil seems to have changed some, don't you think?"

Hailey's attention lurched back to her friend. "I haven't seen much of him, so I wouldn't know."

"I thought he was in charge of the rooftop garden?"

"We've met for business with our partners, not really catching up for old times' sake." Hopefully that sounded innocuous enough. She nibbled the edge of a cookie.

"I always wondered if the two of you would get together."

Hailey sprayed cookie crumbs across the counter. "What? Are you kidding? Basil and me?" She reached for a napkin to wipe up the crumbs.

"Seems like both of you are always looking for someone, and I got to wondering if you might be looking for each other."

Hailey forced a chuckle. "He's really not my type at all." She'd once thought he might be. When they were both wandering far from God.

Adriana sighed. "Fair enough. I'm not really sure where he stands with the Lord, anyway. But you should get out and meet somebody. Do you know Holden Latimer?"

"I don't think so?"

"Myles met him at jiu jitsu. He's a Christian who attends a church downtown. He works at Bank of America."

"Sounds super respectable." And possibly boring, except for the martial arts. Hailey wouldn't be caught dead slashing, kicking, and chopping, or whatever they did in that particular version. She worked up enough sweat in a hot kitchen. No thanks to exertion anytime else.

"He is." Adriana laughed. "But he's a good guy. Myles has brought him home for dinner a few times. You might hit it off with him."

Hmm. Was Hailey really desperate enough to go on a blind date?

"We could have both of you over sometime soon. And a couple of other people so it wouldn't seem forced, if you wanted."

Not quite a blind date. But would everyone Adriana invited know she was setting Hailey up? Did it even matter? "He's probably got a girlfriend." All respectable men her age had settled down already. Wait. She eyed Adriana. "Please tell me he's not twenty-two."

Adriana giggled. "I'm not sure exactly, but he's over thirty. He's kind of cute, too. Blond, curly hair."

"Does Myles know you noticed?" Hailey raised her eyebrows.

"Myles knows he is very, very safe."

What would that kind of confidence feel like? She had no clue. She'd never let anyone get close enough to find out. Not since Venice, and look how that ended.

Maybe a slightly boring but respectable man would be a good idea. Hailey'd had all the passion in those short few weeks that anyone needed for a lifetime. Maybe the best she could hope for the rest of her life might be mutual respect.

She slid a glance at Adriana. "I'd be okay meeting him. Sort of by accident."

"Really?" Adriana's eyes brightened. "I'll get Myles to invite him for dinner again. You want to just drop by and pick something up? I don't know. Tomatoes from the garden or something. And I'll invite you in, and introduce you, and you hang around a few minutes and see how it goes?"

That sounded relatively painless. Also, Holden wasn't Basil, and he wouldn't remind her of him if he looked that different.

Hailey shrugged. "Yeah. Okay. That's workable. I can drop you guys some leftovers from the bakery, whatever we've got that day. Let me know when."

"Perfect. You won't be sorry, Hailey."

"I probably will be."

HOW MANY TIMES could a man jog up and down a set of stairs past a woman's apartment and never run into her?

Dozens, apparently. She was probably hiding from him. Basil could hardly blame her. Past Basil would knock on her door and swagger on in. *Really* Past Basil would have expected some action.

He wasn't that guy anymore or, at least, he was trying not to be. But Hailey pushed his buttons. Every. Single. One. He thought she'd see he'd changed, but maybe it wasn't that obvious.

And there was still the small matter that he'd never apologized for what happened in Italy. For years, he hadn't thought he needed to. Their fling had been totally mutual, yet something had obviously struck Hailey wrong. Otherwise, they'd have picked up in Bridgeview what they'd left off in Venice a couple of months prior. That was totally what he'd expected. Get an apartment together. Go public.

But it was like she'd turned into a nun or something, at least where he was concerned. She turned on the charm for any other guy and twisted the faucet off instantly when he was nearby.

Maybe twelve years was long enough. Maybe he should actually ask her what happened to change her mind and then apologize. Maybe then he could move on. If not with her, then without her.

The little devil with a pitchfork perched on one shoulder laughed his head off at the gullible angel sitting on the other. Basil had spent over half his life listening to the dude with the forked tail, but maybe the one with the halo wasn't as naive as he'd always assumed. Maybe the cherub had it right all along.

Huh.

Apologizing was the worst. Letting anyone see the vulnerable guy inside... ugh. He'd had to with Peter and Jasmine. They'd forgiven him, taken his investment funds, and put him to work. It hadn't been as painful as he'd dreaded. He'd managed to avoid the conversation with his parents or his brothers so far.

But, Hailey. It seemed he'd hurt her the worst, even more than any woman who'd come after her. Hailey was the only one who'd known him *before*. The only one who expected better of him than he'd delivered.

Yeah, he owed Hailey a real apology, but she'd never open the door to him... except she'd be expecting talk about the rooftop garden.

Basil looked over the edge of the roof just in time to see her turn onto the sidewalk that led to the back of the building. It hadn't been his imagination. She'd been out.

He turned to the work crew. "It's too hot. I'm off for the day. See you at dawn."

"Yeah, me, too," one of them said. They gathered up their tools as Basil headed for the stairs. He listened for Hailey's door to close one level down then jogged past and up the street. He needed a quick shower, some clean clothes, and a bundle of wildflowers from the community garden on the next block. He didn't want to waste the time driving downtown to the flower shop. Besides, Hailey would likely throw the bouquet in his face, so there was no reason to waste hard-earned cash.

Half an hour later, he stood at her door again, with the flowers behind his back.

Hailey pulled open the door at his knock. "Basil. What do you want?" Her face was blank. Impassive.

"I need to talk to you for a few minutes."

"If this is about the rooftop, can it wait until tomorrow?"

"It's not."

She narrowed her gaze at him. "There's nothing else we need to talk about."

"I think there is." Basil thrust the daisies into her hands. "Please."

"No. There's nothing to say." She pushed them back toward him.

Basil shoved his hands in his shorts pockets. "Torre dell'Orologio at sunset."

She refused to allow memories of the clocktower on Piazza San Marco back into her head. "You're playing dirty."

"I played dirty then. Now I'm trying to come clean."

"It's not possible." She still held the flowers away from herself as though they might be hiding a tarantula.

"Please let me come in. You can explain why you hate me. I'll apologize and grovel or whatever it takes. You'll enjoy seeing that part. Then I'll leave and never bother you again."

"I'm not explaining anything."

Basil's eyebrows shot up. "With a statement like that, I think you need to. You left me high and dry, Hailey. When you kissed me goodbye in front of Marco Polo Airport, I—"

"Shh." She glanced down the stairs. "Don't talk about that in public."

"Let me come inside."

"No."

If that's how she wanted to play it... He ratcheted up the volume. "When you kissed me goodbye—"

Hailey grabbed his shirt, hauled him through the door, and slammed it shut. "What are you trying to prove?" she hissed.

"Mission accomplished." Basil straightened his mussed-up T-shirt.

"I hate you. You know that?"

"It's been kind of hard to miss, but I don't know why."

She flounced into the kitchen and flung the flowers into the garbage can under her sink. "You're impossible. And not very bright."

"Enlighten me." He followed her and blocked the doorway.

Hailey glared at him but, wait — was that a tear? Oh, man. Not only a tear, but her jaw was quivering. Great. Basil wasn't equipped to deal with this. Maybe a quick prayer for wisdom wouldn't go amiss about now, if God was listening to the likes of him.

Basil prayed. Watched the emotions play across her face. Waited.

Her shoulders began to convulse. She dashed away more tears.

That didn't mean she wanted a hug. He'd likely get slugged if he touched her. More waiting. He was not a patient man, but he owed her this, at least.

"Have you ever heard of consequences?" she managed between sobs.

Basil nodded. Pretty sure he'd met those during his month in lockup for drunk driving and attempting to run a roadblock.

"Well, you didn't have any. I got them all."

"What?" Why wouldn't she stop being all emotional, leave off the coded lingo, and just tell him what she meant?

"I got pregnant in Venice, Basil."

He reeled and grabbed the doorframe to hold him up. "You what? We used protection."

"Condoms are only 98% effective. Which is not the same as 100%."

Duh. But the look on her face stopped his snippy reply. Hailey wasn't making this up. He'd bet his bottom dollar on that. "Where's my child?" She must have adopted it out. Maybe Basil could find him or her.

The anguish in her eyes hardened, and he knew before she told him. "I aborted."

"No." He leaned heavily on the doorframe.

"Yes." Hailey closed her eyes for a few seconds. "My mother—"

"That was a living human being, Hailey." His voice came

out harsher then intended. But how could he soften his response after a bomb like that one?

"You think I don't know that?"

"I would have married you."

She scoffed. "Right. I was eighteen, Basil. Just out of high school."

"Dafne was only sixteen."

"So, your cousin was a paragon who went through being pregnant her senior year and kept her baby to raise alone. She had her parents' support. Didn't you hear me? My parents advised me to get rid of it. They were in some sensitive talks involving the papal office, and it would all have been ruined."

"That was more important than their own daughter? Their own grandchild?" His voice only continued to rise.

"To them, yes!"

"Hailey."

"Don't 'Hailey' me. You weren't there. I did what I had to do at the time. Do I regret it? Sure, I do. *Of course, I do.* But nothing will bring that baby back, Basil Santoro, so don't you get off on judging me."

"I wasn't judg—"

"You were, too. Everyone would, if they knew." Hailey covered her face with both hands, her whole body shaking. "You can show yourself out now."

He didn't even want to hug her anymore. Didn't want to comfort her or console her. How could she have done that? His kid would be twelve now, the same age as Marco's eldest. Or, wait, eleven. Or something. He'd never done pregnancy math before.

Had he been ready to be a husband and father? Heck, no. But they'd have managed, somehow. The cold truth washed over him. They'd have been divorced by now if that's how it had been.

"Go," she whispered.

He steeled himself against her anguish. "I came here to apologize for being a jerk, but I never dreamed you were hiding something this big for so many years."

Hailey's hands flew to her sides, and she advanced toward him, her eyes blazing. "I'm sorry, okay?" Her voice was cold. Precise. "This is an apology."

Basil staggered back a few steps. "I'll need to think about it."

"Get out."

7

*A*driana was determined. Hailey'd give her that. They'd talked, what, Monday morning? And Wednesday afternoon, Adriana texted to say Holden was coming for dinner.

That agreement had been before she'd dumped everything on Basil and he'd walked away, coldly furious. What had she expected? Him to be understanding and supportive? Yeah, right.

Like he had any grounds to judge her. He'd had a drinking problem. He'd been to jail. He'd probably slept with dozens of women since that summer in Venice.

What Hailey had done had been legal, which didn't make it right. She wasn't stupid enough to think it did.

She didn't want to be set up with some boring banker or anyone else, for that matter. She wanted to go back in time and shake some sense into the infatuated girl she'd been. Not just the abortion, but the whole thing with Basil.

She'd decided to see Venice while her parents were in Rome with their diplomatic meetings. Basil had spent a few weeks with Marietta's family in Tuscany and was doing some sightseeing on his own before returning to the US.

They'd run into each other quite by accident at St. Mark's Basilica. Bam. Instant connection. She was no longer just a friend of his kid sister. They'd spent every day together and quite a few nights. Her parents were thankful she was out of their hair, not distracting them during their mission.

Their attitude had certainly changed a couple of weeks after Basil returned home, and she'd missed her period. Suddenly, Mom was all hands-on, demanding where they'd gone wrong.

Hello? How about when they left their only child behind with her grandparents because their duties were too important to be sidelined? How about when she'd always known she was an accident they'd regretted?

And then, how *dare* she be an embarrassment and a hindrance to their mission?

How dare they email out of the blue and tell her they were coming for a visit this fall? She hadn't seen them for four or five years. When she had need of parental figures, she spent a weekend with Kass's dad and stepmom. It was amazing how little ambition Uncle Farrell had compared to his brother, Hailey's father.

Hailey wasn't a quitter. Thanks to her grandparents, Bridgeview was her home, but she'd never wished so much that she could take a suitcase and run as right now.

Maybe a vacation wasn't completely out of the question. Could Reina and Julissa handle the kitchen for a few weeks? Hailey probably needed more staff.

Not that she could go anywhere now with the rooftop garden in progress and her parents coming in a few weeks.

After seeing Basil every day on the project and time with Mom and Dad, she'd be ready for that escape. Desperately.

Cancun sounded good. Definitely not Europe.

Hailey's phone chimed again.

Adriana: RU in?

Hailey: If it will get you off my back, okay.

Adriana: Haha. Cya 7-8.

Whatever. She'd meet the guy. He'd be as boring as expected, and that would be the end.

When the bistro closed at five, Hailey went downstairs. Kass and a few employees were still cleaning up and prepping for tomorrow.

"Hey!" Kass grinned at her from ringing off the cash register. "How was your afternoon?"

"Good. I'm going over to Adriana's tonight and promised dessert. What have we got around?"

Basil's cousin Gabriella paused as she took a tray out of the display case. "No cinnamon rolls, that's for sure. We ran out at four. But there are brownies and lemon bars and a few other random things."

Guys tended to go for citrus before chocolate. "The lemon bars sound perfect. But maybe I'll help myself to one of those brownies for now."

"Chocoholic as always." Kass laughed. "Hey, I'll walk home with you if you can wait a few minutes. What time is Adriana expecting you?"

"Oh, that's okay. I'm going later, after dinner."

Kass looked at her quizzically. "I thought... never mind."

Hailey snagged a brownie. "It's all good." Not that her cousin would believe her, since she couldn't seem to hold eye contact. "Heard from your dad and Lenore lately?"

"We're going to visit the farm this weekend. Sebastian is so excited. Want to come along?"

And sit in the backseat with two kids? No, thanks. Hailey shook her head. "Not this time."

Kass glanced at Gabriella and back. Hailey'd get a grilling if the younger woman wasn't in the room. She could tell.

They'd employed way too many Santoro cousins over the past six years. That's what they got for hiring locals right when the younger group was hitting that age. Gabriella was the last of them, but she wouldn't work for them much longer since she was nearly through college. Dafne had never worked here much. She'd been too busy with her little boy.

Just as well. Hailey couldn't have denied Dafne a job, but she hated every reminder that the girl had taken the path of life while Hailey had not. Sure, their situations were different, but there was no excuse.

And with no excuse came no forgiveness.

Hailey knew better. God forgave everything. She'd read the first chapter of First John. But she'd been so deliberate in her choice to obey her mother and ignore the Spirit of God. Granted, her faith had been shallow at best at the time, but the fact was, she'd known better.

"Earth to Hailey?"

She blinked to see Kass's hand waving in front of her face. "What?"

"You totally spaced out. You've been doing that a lot lately. Are you okay?"

"Sure, I'm fine!" She poured a little extra enthusiasm into her voice. Added a wide grin.

Kass's eyebrows shot up.

Too much? She'd tone it back. "Seriously, it's all good."

"Okay. If you say so." Kass glanced toward Gabriella, who'd set the box of lemon squares on the counter and was now flipping chairs upside-down onto the tables so they could sweep and mop.

Hailey picked up the box. "Give Sebastian and Eleanor a kiss from me."

"In the words of a nine-year-old, ewww."

She laughed and headed out the back door.

BASIL'S THIGHS BURNED. It'd been a few years since he'd done a lot of cycling, but today had called for some major physical exertion. Cycling had brought him into Myles Sheridan's sphere — the guy was crazy fit for a teacher. Probably pedaled twenty miles before breakfast six days a week.

It was a rare cool day for August, so Myles had jumped when Basil called him. Soon school would be back in session and Myles wouldn't be free to drop everything.

They coasted side by side down the hill into Bridgeview, and Basil pulled out his water bottle for a drink. Empty.

Myles chuckled. "Come on in for iced tea before you go home."

"Nah, I'm a sweaty mess."

"Me, too. Don't worry about it. Unless you've got something cold at home?"

Past Basil would have had a fridge full of beer. Present Basil didn't even have any ice made. Who knew not all fridges froze little cubes automatically? He'd been spoiled, because this rental unit had a very basic fridge.

"If you're sure."

Myles shoulder-checked and veered into his driveway. "Come on."

Basil followed him and dismounted before his bike stopped. He unbuckled his helmet, slung the straps over the handlebars, and followed Myles into the house.

Adriana met Myles with a kiss on the lips that made Basil wish for things that could never be his. Then she seemed to notice him. "Basil! Hi."

"I offered him some iced tea. We've got time, right?"

Basil's brows shot up.

"Sure, but you need a shower before Holden gets here. In case you didn't know." She left the room. "Violet! Is Jamie with you?"

Myles laughed. "I'm well aware," he called to his wife's retreating back then beckoned Basil into the kitchen and retrieved a jug from the fridge.

"If you guys are having company over..." Although, when weren't they? Adriana lived to entertain.

"It's just Holden Latimer." Myles poured two tall glasses. "Do you know him?"

"I don't think so."

"He's in my jiu jitsu class. Nice guy."

"Cool."

"You'd like him. You should stay for dinner."

Basil laughed and shook his head. "If you need a shower first, I definitely do."

"You live two blocks away. Drink up. You have plenty of time to go home and come back."

"Nah."

"Come on. We can shoot some hoops afterward."

Basil snickered. "I didn't know you liked basketball."

"A guy can't live in Bridgeview and gain any respect without it, or so I've learned. Still, no one has asked me to play with the Santoro Bulldogs during Hoopfest."

Basil snorted. The cousins got pretty intense about the annual three-on-three competition downtown, placing high in the standings some years. Hoopfest was one of the things Basil had missed most while living in Seattle. The camaraderie of the Bulldogs as they trained hard for competition. On the court, basketball chops were all that mattered. Not a guy's standing in the clan or where he worked or whether he had a girlfriend or anything but scoring baskets.

"Basil's staying for dinner," Myles announced. "There's lots, right?"

Adriana stood in the archway, her jaw dropping. She started to speak a couple of times before finally managing, "Holden's coming over."

"Right." Myles put the jug back in the fridge. "I think he and Basil would hit it off. They have a lot in common. Besides, Basil needs to get to know some people he's not related to. No offense against the Santoro clan, of course."

Adriana bit her lip and glanced between them.

How could Myles not notice his wife's body language? But the guy was oblivious.

"We're eating at six, man." Myles gulped his iced tea. "I'll go get that shower then give you a hand, honey. Whatever you need."

"I'm not doing anything fancy. Just grilled burgers and a couple of salads."

Myles kissed Adriana's cheek. "What's for dessert?"

Adriana opened her mouth and closed it again before glancing at Basil. She closed her eyes for a second. "Hailey's bringing it over later."

"Oh, cool. I hope it's cinnamon rolls." Myles backed out of the kitchen, pointing at Basil. "See you back here shortly."

Leaving Basil with Adriana. "It's okay. I don't have to come." But his brain was buzzing. What was going on?

Her smile looked more genuine this time. "Myles is right. I think you and Holden would like each other."

The words, "but Hailey," formed on his lips but didn't come out.

It was doubtful that Adriana knew the whole story or guessed that Basil and Hailey had been an item way back when. No one had ever mentioned a thing about that summer to him. He'd never told, and it sure seemed like Hailey hadn't, either. Not after her blurted reveal a couple of days ago.

That had shaken his foundation to its core. To be honest, his foundation had been a wreck for a long time. Years.

"Seriously. It's just a casual meal with a friend, and Myles invited you. It's fine. Great, actually."

Basil searched her face, but there was no hint of that earlier hesitation. Still, she'd mentioned Hailey was coming by and bringing dessert.

A lightbulb went off in Basil's head. Adriana wanted Holden and Hailey to meet, and Myles had no clue. That's what was going on.

He grinned at her. "Thanks. I'd love to. I was going to hit a drive-through later..."

"Ugh." She wrinkled her nose. "That's disgusting. Please, come."

"I will. Your burgers are way better."

No comparison.

8

*T*he banker wasn't half bad.

Basil wouldn't mind considering Holden a friend, but that was out of the question since the other guy had designs on Hailey North. Or did he? While Basil noted Adriana's deck chair gave her a good view of their backyard's street entrance, Holden was fully engaged in showing twelve-year-old Sam some jiu jitsu moves, apparently oblivious that anyone might drop by.

"Not like that, Sam." Ten-year-old Violet gave a medal-worthy eyeroll. "Put your back into it."

Sam barely spared his sister a glance before grappling with Holden again. Holden swept in and tossed the boy over his shoulder with a flamboyant twirl just as Adriana surged to her feet, dumping Jamie into Myles's lap.

Basil had been smart enough to position himself with a similar view to Adriana's, but he'd allowed himself to become distracted for a few seconds.

Now Hailey stepped through the gate, carrying a box from the bakery.

And she was gorgeous. She'd gone all-out for this occasion in casually dressy silk shorts and a lacy top that made Basil itch to tug her close. Her blond hair had a little extra bounce, flipping up at the tips, and she'd spent more care than usual on her makeup.

Basil's blood ran cold. She'd known Holden would be here. She was putting out the effort for Holden, not him. And Holden was still absorbed with his demonstration.

Hailey stopped just inside the gate, gaze focused on the banker and the pre-teen. What did she see in the man? Anything? Maybe she appreciated a guy who wasn't too important to hang out with a kid.

A kid about the same age as their son or daughter would have been.

She'd had no right to abort his child.

He'd had no right to claim her body in Venice.

She'd been right there with him every step, every dance. They'd tossed all caution to the wind except for those dratted condoms that apparently weren't as foolproof as he'd been led to believe.

"Hi, Hailey!" Adriana bounded toward her.

Hailey's gaze swung toward the back deck, but her wide smile froze when she found Basil.

He leaned back into his chair, gave her a little wave, and bobbed his eyebrows in her direction.

She thrust the box at Adriana. "Sorry, I can't stay. Kass and I..." Her voice faltered.

Hailey wasn't very good at lying on her feet. It seemed she couldn't think of anything quickly enough.

"Hailey!" he called. "What's in that box?"

"None of your business," she shot back.

From beside him, Myles chuckled. "She's a firecracker, that one."

Hard to argue.

Holden set Sam right-side up on the grass, finally noticing Hailey. Was the flush on the guy's cheeks from exertion or from the realization he'd been set up? Because, from where Basil sat, he'd wager a guess the banker hadn't known about the setup any more than Myles had.

Crossing his arms over his chest, Basil plastered on his trademark sardonic grin. He'd do a little steering of his own. It would never do for Hailey to actually fall for the blond banker.

Jealous? Basil blinked at the thought. Nah. Why should he be? What he and Hailey'd had had been over years ago.

Besides, she'd killed his baby.

What kind of guy hadn't checked in a month or two later? Had simply wallowed for more than a decade, treating his ex as distantly as she treated him? What kind of guy didn't try to figure out why the change?

A guy like him. Full of himself. He'd figured she wanted to play hard-to-get after the fact, so whatever. He could show her what she was missing. What she could have continued to have.

Yeah, that had gone over well.

He'd been stupid, but she was the murderer, not him.

"Holden, I'd like you to meet Hailey North, a friend of mine. Hailey and her cousin own Bridgeview Bakery and Bistro on West Main toward downtown. Hailey, Holden's in Myles's jiu jitsu class as you might be able to tell from how he's manhandling Sam over there. He's a loans officer at Bank of America."

"Pleased to meet you." Holden extended a hand, and Adriana plucked the bakery box from Hailey's grasp so Hailey was free to shake it.

"It's nice to meet you, as well." Hailey's voice was so soft Basil strained to hear it. "I just dropped by with some lemon squares that were leftover at work today. I know they're Myles's favorite."

Basil noted she didn't try to explain how she hadn't known Holden would be here. "Hey, lemon squares are great," he called. "Do I get one?"

Adriana opened the box. "Looks like there are plenty." But she extended it toward Holden. "Hailey's a fabulous baker as well as a great cook."

Gag. Did Adriana have to lay it on so thick?

Hailey looked down, and... were her eyelashes actually fluttering? Good grief.

"Hey, looks good." Holden flashed a grin at Hailey as he lifted out a square.

She smiled back at him.

Enough, already. Basil surged to his feet and jogged down the steps toward the group. He slung an arm over Hailey's shoulder as Sam helped himself to a piece. "Oh, Hailey, you've been holding out. These look amazing." He gave her a squeeze and reached in. "You are a wizard in the kitchen."

Hailey shrugged out from under his arm, shifted to the other side of Adriana, and focused on Holden. "Sam's pretty good at jiu jitsu, isn't he?"

"He is not," Violet sputtered. "I can take him."

Adriana ruffled her daughter's hair, but Violet ducked away. "Well, I can."

Hailey chuckled. "I'm sure you could, but maybe Holden just taught Sam a killer move that will make him the winner."

Sam puffed out his chest and eyed his sister.

Holden laughed. "I've seen them at the club dozens of times. They're both excellent." He took a bite then saluted Hailey with the square. "Amazing. Lemon anything is my favorite."

Mine, too. But saying it out loud right now would scream of vying for Hailey's attention. No way was Basil about to exhibit desperation in front of the banker. Calm, cool, and collected was his thing, as though nothing mattered.

Problem was, he cared. After twelve years, he'd been ready to make his apologies and claim his girl. It was like she'd been waiting for him to get his stuff together.

He absolutely hadn't counted on her moving on with Holden Latimer under Basil's very eye.

⌒‿⌒

HAILEY FLASHED a smile at Myles's friend. Adriana had only hinted at the man's good looks, and the fact he was willing to work out with a twelve-year-old only stood in his favor.

But how could Adriana have shafted her like this by inviting Basil? That was totally not playing fair. Hailey had agreed to meet Holden, and it was extremely awkward with Basil hanging around and pretending he had a right to hug her.

Besides, wasn't Basil still angry at her? She didn't dare look at him long enough to try to read his eyes or body language. He was way too practiced at that don't-care facade — a quick glance would tell her nothing but would let him know he was getting to her.

All she could do was step closer to Holden. "Have you been doing jiu-jitsu long?"

"Since I was a kid, younger than Sam here."

"I'm younger than Sam," announced Violet. "And I've been in jiu-jitsu since I was five."

Sheesh, Basil was the least of Hailey's problems. She couldn't shake Adriana's kids, either.

"How about you?" Holden's appreciative gaze ran the length of Hailey's body and back to her face. "What's your favorite way to stay fit?"

"I... uh, I'm pretty busy."

He smiled. "Whatever you're doing is working for you."

"Mostly running stairs, honestly." And standing for eight hours at a stretch, but that didn't sound so impressive.

Holden's face lit up. "How many flights per set is your goal?"

Flights... set... goal... what was he talking about? Oh, boy, she'd made him think she did it for fitness, not survival.

Basil snickered.

Hailey resisted the urge to skewer him with a glare. "Like I said, I'm pretty busy with work. I start in the kitchen at four, and I'm on my feet for eight hours, often more. Some days it's all I can do to stagger up the stairs and collapse in front of the television when I'm done."

"Oh." Holden's smile visibly faded. "I have such a sedentary job that I need all the help I can get staying in shape. Besides, I love it."

Why had Adriana thought this man might be a good fit for her again? Right, at thirty, Hailey couldn't afford to be quite as choosy. A single man about her age, a Christian with a decent job... but, still. The real problem was that Hailey hadn't been picky enough at eighteen. That summer in Italy had been a disaster from one end to the other. She should have known, even then, that Basil Santoro didn't have staying power, that he could never be the man she needed to be a stable part of her future.

Hailey turned her back on the rest of the group and focused on Holden. "Tell me more about your job. It sounds interesting." Which was a total lie, but that didn't mean he was a boring guy all around. It wasn't like she'd be going to the office with him, even if they ended up together.

She didn't want to end up with Holden. She still craved Basil, but she absolutely needed to get that weakness out of her system. On paper, there was nothing wrong with Holden.

He shrugged and tossed her a grin. "It's boring as all get out. I live for five o'clock, when my real life begins. I plug numbers into a computer all day long. I don't even get to make decisions about who deserves a loan and who doesn't. It's all up to the computer — I just get to deliver the news in person and oversee signing contracts as they're approved."

"There's not much computerized about baking sourdough bread and cinnamon rolls." Hailey kept her smile in place. "My job is all about the feel and innate knowledge."

"I'll have to stop by sometime and check out your place." Holden polished off the last bite of lemon square. "If this is anything to go by, a guy could gain fifty pounds frequenting your bistro."

"We offer some sugar-free, grain-free options as well." She hated giving Astrid any credit.

"Interesting." He leaned closer. "I'm a sugar-lover at heart."

"Me, too." Hailey held out the box. "Why don't you take the rest of these home when you go? I think everyone who wants one has had a chance already."

"You sure?"

"Of course." She took a deep breath and managed an eyelash-flutter. "That will remind you to stop by the bistro sometime soon. I'll be in the kitchen — be sure to say hi when you come in."

She heard a coughing sound from Basil's general direction, but there was no way she was acknowledging him.

Holden reached for the box, his gaze intent on hers. His fingers touched hers and lingered. He lowered his voice. "Thanks, Hailey. Hey, want to go out sometime? We could hit Riverside Park and try the SkyRide if you like."

"Sounds fun. I've never ridden that gondola." Shouldn't she feel something with their hands in contact? Even touching her stainless-steel mixer was more thrilling. Maybe she'd used up all her feels on Basil when she was eighteen. "I work Tuesday through Saturday."

"How about Sunday afternoon? What time's good?"

"Any time after two, maybe?" She lowered her voice. "My card is in the box."

He flashed her a dimpled smile. "Now that's thinking. I'll give you a call later." He glanced past her as though measuring their onlookers. "I should get going. I'm meeting a buddy for a run along Centennial Trail shortly."

"Sounds fun." No. It did not, but it still seemed the thing to say, at least if she wanted Holden to like her. And she did want that, if only so she could prove to Basil that someone found her attractive. Someone without all the baggage.

Holden said his goodbyes all around, mussed up Sam's hair, and waved as he headed out the gate.

Hailey took a deep breath and turned to the group, avoiding Basil's knowing gaze. She raised her eyebrows at Adriana. Her friend had some explaining to do.

Basil retreated to the deck and resumed his seat, leaning toward Myles and tickling the toddler on his lap. Hopefully, Basil was out of range.

Hailey took Adriana's arm and towed her toward the lower part of the yard. "Why is Basil here?"

"He and Myles were cycling together just before dinner, and Myles invited him."

"You could have warned me."

Adriana pulled her arm away and turned to look at Hailey. "Why? What's the problem with Basil?"

Hailey opened her mouth and closed it again. Too much protesting would only trigger Adriana's suspicions. "I just didn't expect anyone here but your family."

"You told me you didn't like Basil."

"I never said that. Of course, I like him. Just not romantically."

"Then it shouldn't matter. What if Alex had been here?"

"Alex is married."

"What difference does that make? I'm talking about someone being around to witness you and Holden meeting. Just some random man from Bridgeview."

"You set me up."

"You agreed to it. And it looks like you and Holden hit it off, regardless."

Hailey took a deep breath and let it out slowly. "He seems nice."

Adriana nudged Hailey with her elbow. "Told you."

"You did." But nice wasn't going to cut it. It wasn't even that the guy seemed fitness crazy, Hailey's total opposite. They could overcome that if there were a spark. On an attraction scale of one to ten, Holden landed at a solid one.

Basil, on the other hand, scored eleven, and *that* was a problem she didn't want to think about.

asil." Nonna clutched both his cheeks and gave them a tight squeeze. "You have not been to see me since your return."

"Uh, I've been busy?" He gave his grandmother an awkward pat and tried to pull away, but she hadn't relinquished her grip yet.

"You should never be too busy for family. Why did you return to Bridgeview if not to make an old woman happy?"

A thousand other reasons, most of them named Hailey. "I always intended to come back. I needed to save up some money."

"There are jobs here." She peered into his eyes.

How did she even do that when she was probably eight inches shorter than him? Basil grasped her wrists and gently disengaged her grip. Whew. That was better. "I had to make my own way."

Nonna shook her head. "That is not so. You need to find God's way and walk in it."

He managed a grin, much easier without her hands

squeezing his face. "Hey, I was in church this morning. I even remember what Tomas preached about."

"Sitting in a pew does not make you a Christian any more than sitting on my kitchen counter makes a tomato into ragu."

"I'm a Christian."

Nonna's face softened. "I recall you praying with your mamma when you were a wee one. But what have you done since then to grow as a believer?"

Wow, Nonna pulled no punches. Basil grimaced. "Not much, for a long time. But I'm working on it, okay?" He patted her shoulder and glanced over at his mother. "Need a hand, Mom?"

Family dinner was tradition on Sundays after church. Basil's brothers and sister and their families would all be arriving within minutes. He'd take Marco's boys out and shoot some hoops while others prepped lunch. Basil had missed enough of their life. Caden had even played on a youth team comprised of Bridgeview kids in Hoopfest this year.

Basil pushed the thought of his own child out of his mind. His anger had bubbled like a witch's cauldron for a few days, but it was down to a simmer. How could he blame Hailey for the decision she'd made when she so clearly wasn't over it herself? He'd abandoned her, assuming if he beckoned her with his little finger she'd return. He'd treated her abominably.

Still did.

Ouch.

His dad said something, and Basil blinked his parents' dining room back into focus. Evan jogged up the stairs from the basement. Basil had lived down there for far too long, too, but at least his baby brother was still in college and would make something of his life when he finally graduated.

The front door opened behind Basil, and Alex ushered in Marley, both of them laughing as they gave each other a lingering, loving look.

Envy was a real thing. Maybe Basil should have stayed in Seattle like the coward he really was. No. Nonna was right. He needed to quit the pretense and grow up. He'd already taken the first steps, but he'd faltered at Hailey's news. Not completely true. He'd been faltering already. Being back in Bridgeview presented him with all his previous patterns. It would be far easier to stay the Basil he'd been than push himself — hard — to make new decisions.

But... he had to.

He couldn't let Hailey derail him. He was thirty-three years old, and people still saw him as a kid like he saw Evan. But his youngest brother was, what, twenty-five now? Marco had already been a father of two at that age.

Basil needed to adjust. Figure out how to become a responsible adult. He could start by forgiving Hailey. By asking her to forgive him. His gut rebelled at the thought. What she'd done was unforgivable. And yet... he hadn't treated her well, either. He was no saint himself.

No one was. *For all have sinned.* Yeah, he knew the verse. Knew the Bible's teaching on the topic.

A hand clapped on his shoulder, and Basil pivoted to see his older brother.

"Lost in thought?"

"I guess." Basil huffed a laugh.

Marco poked his head at the door. "The boys are hoping you'll take them on out there."

Basketball with Marco's kids meant all three against

Uncle Basil. That was fine. He could take them with one hand tied behind his back and love every minute. He grinned. "They've got it."

"Bro, you should come for dinner one night. When are you free?"

Basil chuckled. When was he busy was the better question. "Sounds good. Anytime. Up to you and Daria."

His sister-in-law gave him a quick hug. "Tuesday? We can't wait to hear all about what you're doing with Hailey and Kass's building."

"It's coming along well, considering we only started a week ago." And considering that Hailey had spent most of that time avoiding him. How could he blame her?

"Bring photos and deets. Dinner's at six."

"Thanks." He meant it. This whole family vibe felt foreign and familiar at the same time. Was that even possible? But if anyone could help him find firm footing, it would be them. If only he dared open up completely and let someone in.

Was it enough to do that with Jesus? It didn't seem to be. Basil remembered the words, but they didn't seem enough. He'd made some first steps by returning home, but truly making amends would take more groveling than he'd been able to manage yet. Was that the magic wand he'd been missing?

Ugh. He didn't know. But for now, he'd just get outside and score a bunch of baskets against his punky nephews.

꩜

BESIDE HER, Holden stretched to see the lineup. He grimaced. "We're not the only ones who thought this was a fun thing to do on a Sunday afternoon. You want to stick it out or go do something else?"

"We don't have to, if you don't want to." She'd never ridden the gondola over the river before for good reason. Heights were so not her friend, and the churning water beneath them only added to her nervousness. "Have you done it lots of times?"

"A few." He shrugged. "It's cool, but it's not that exciting. Not like skydiving."

"Uh, yeah. I'm never doing that."

Holden grinned, his dimple showing. "Never say never."

"Oh, I can absolutely, indubitably say *never* to that one."

"Where's your spirit of adventure?"

"I left it in—" Yeah, not talking about Italy with this guy. "A box somewhere," she finished lamely.

"You'll have to dig it out." He bobbed his eyebrows as he leaned closer.

Hailey crossed her arms over her chest and took a step back, right on the toes of the teen waiting behind her. "Sorry!"

"Watch where you're going, lady."

Holden took her arm and glowered at the boy. "She said she was sorry. And you're crowding her."

The kid scowled. "Am not. This place is packed."

Hailey glanced up the line. They'd moved closer since arriving twenty minutes ago, but it was going to be a while yet with only fifteen cabins on the cables. She sure didn't want to share one with the teens behind them.

"We could just take the sidewalk along the falls," she suggested. She knew she was a chicken, but solid cement under her feet sounded better than dangling and swaying above the rapids.

"We could do that afterward and get another perspective." Holden strained to see the line again. "We'll probably get on pretty soon, though. You'll like it."

Promise? But Hailey kept the comment to herself. She'd steeled herself for this ride. How could she even call herself a Spokanite if she'd never partaken of the local attractions? Holden wouldn't likely ride the Looff carousel with her, but it was more her speed than the SkyRide.

Holden's fingers wrapped around hers as they moved up in the line. That seemed a little fresh. She snuck a glance at him, and he grinned down at her. This relationship was either going to be spectacular or a dud. Probably a dud. She should never have agreed to Adriana's ploy to get her to start dating. At the very least, she should pick her own guys.

That had gone over so well for her in the past. Memories of the beach at Lido di Venezia poked at her consciousness, but she slammed the lid back down on them and clutched Holden's hand. She was going to get over Basil, once and for all, if it killed her. And it might.

Holden slipped his arm around her waist as though her grip had given him permission. Maybe it had. How should she know current dating rules? She held as still as she could, not melting against him and not pulling away, as they approached the loading platform.

How he managed to get the two of them alone in one cabin, she didn't know, but soon he sat beside her on one side of the wobbling car.

"Should I sit on the other side? It feels off balance."

"No worries." He tucked his arm around her shoulders again and drew her against him.

The guy was awfully hands-on for a first date. Probably her imagination, though.

The cabin pulled forward and stopped again, swaying. Hailey almost held in a gasp.

"It stops a lot," Holden said, glancing at the car behind them as the teens got onboard.

"Good to know."

A few minutes later the gondola stopped above the river. Hailey held rigid, barely daring to look at the rushing falls beneath them. Good thing this wasn't springtime when the river was swollen with snowmelt from the mountains. There was plenty enough going on below the SkyRide as it was.

Holden's warm hand massaged her upper arm. Maybe he'd sensed her discomfort and was trying to help her relax. It wasn't quite working, but she'd give him an A for effort.

She gave him a wobbly smile.

His mouth descended on hers, and she pushed away. "What? No!"

"What do you mean, no?" His eyebrows tightened.

"I meant get your lips off me." Hailey surged to the facing seat. The whole cabin rocked with her scramble, or maybe it was only that the gondola was in motion again.

"Oh, good grief, Hailey. That was a *come here* look if I ever saw one."

"You're wrong."

"At least now I know why you're still single at thirty."

She straightened her spine. "And I know why you are, too. Women deserve more respect. And I definitely expected better from a Christian."

Holden rolled his eyes. "It's not like I was trying to rape you. It was only a little kiss. No big deal."

Had she over-reacted? Possibly, but the point remained. "Perhaps not to you, but you didn't ask."

"Well, sor-*ree*."

Hailey gripped the edge of the hard plastic seat with both hands. This date had gone south in record time. See if she let any of her friends set her up ever again.

Blergh. Adriana would ask how it went, and Hailey wasn't about to lie. It would be a temptation, except for Adriana would still think Holden was worthy of one of her friends. He so was not.

Right now, he turned in his seat and stared out the side, the firm jaw she'd admired now looking obstinate instead of attractive. They rode in silence under the iconic bridge, hovered near a graffiti-laden concrete wall, and finally — *finally* — began the return trip.

As the cabin in front of them disgorged its passengers, Hailey gave Holden another hard stare. "Thank you for the gondola ride. The rest of your plans will need to be canceled, though. I'll walk home."

"Look, Hailey, I said I'm sorry."

"And I said this date is over, and there won't be another." The door slid open. Hailey surged out, nearly stumbling as her feet met the unmoving platform.

"Hailey, wait."

She shook her head and plowed through the waiting crowd. If he wouldn't leave her alone now, she'd flag down park patrol. She was so done with Holden Latimer.

Hailey was so, so done with men in general. What about her gave off the easy vibe? From Basil to Holden, that's what guys seemed to think. Yeah, sure, she flirted a bit here and there, but not with either of *them*, just the dozens of innocuous, uninterested men in between.

She and Basil had connected so solidly in Venice that flirtation would have been superfluous. And she hadn't turned on the charm for Holden, either, not with Adriana's family and Basil looking on.

Might as well face it. She'd only ever fallen for one guy, and that had begun badly and ended worse her eighteenth summer. She was forever scarred, and no decent man would ever want her. Could she even tell a prospective spouse about her ordeal? No. That summer was gone. Buried, never to be resurrected.

Hailey glanced over her shoulder as she strode down the sidewalk toward Bridgeview, hugging her clutch against her side. No sign of Holden. It seemed he'd gotten the hint, which was just as well.

Okay, fine. She'd managed on her own for thirty years with little interference from her parents, but her grandparents had loved her. She had one great cousin and a flourishing business. That was enough. She'd pour herself into Bridgeview Bakery and Bistro and build it into the dining destination she knew it could be.

That rooftop patio was key.

Her resolve deflated. It also meant Basil Santoro was going to be part of her life for the next few weeks. By then, her parents would be visiting.

Maybe instead of ferocious work, she needed that vacation she'd been dreaming about the other day.

Now, where was a destination as far removed from Venice as possible?

10

The vision in Basil's head was starting to come together, but how long could Hailey avoid coming up to the rooftop? He'd come early and hung around late, puttering, more days than he could count, but it was like she had a sixth sense of when he was up top. He often walked the few blocks from his apartment to the bistro, so there wasn't a telltale vehicle most of the time.

Soon the door to the inside stairs, along with the mechanical area, would be hidden behind a trellised wall, but it was still in plain view. Basil didn't miss the fact that he oriented his body so the door was within sight wherever he worked.

Today, Uncle Dino had begun installing lines for automatically watering the plants while Basil's crew turned to the surfacing. They'd chosen a recycled-plastic planking to withstand the weather and ordered lightweight concrete planters.

With the bustle of several workers and the buzzing of saws and drills, he saw the door edge open, and there she was. With Kass. The two of them looked around the rooftop, eyes wide.

Kass spotted him. "Basil, this looks amazing."

"It's coming along well." He rose, rolling his shoulders, and turned to Hailey. "What do you think?"

"It's getting easier to imagine the finished space."

"It is, at that." Not everyone had the ability to look at the plans and imagine it in 3-D, even with the extra drawings he'd done. "Zeke's crew is setting pavers on the outside staircase today. Come on over and have a look."

"Oh, we don't want to take up your time." Hailey's protest cut short when Kass towed her toward the roof's eastern edge.

"No problem." Basil fell into step beside her, ready to catch her if she tripped over one of the many tools or supplies littering the surface. "Making sure you're satisfied is my primary concern."

Hailey glanced at him, startled, and he winked. She glowered and stumbled over the end of a stack of water pipes.

He caught her elbow to keep her from falling. "Easy now."

"I'm fine." She jerked away, nearly running into the next pile.

"Oh, that staircase is brilliant!" Kass called from a few yards away. "I love the design, like a castle turret. It looks like it's been there forever. I love how it's open to the elements but still inaccessible to anyone who's not coming through the building."

Sort of like Hailey. Seemingly open yet locked away. He sidled closer. "How was your date with Holden?" Sue him. He needed to know.

She glowered at him. "None of your business."

"When's the next one? Or have you already gone out a few times?"

"There is no next one."

His heart inexplicably leaped in his chest. Maybe he still had a chance. Did he want one, or was he like the dog in the old fable that spitefully laid in the manger so the cows couldn't eat, while the hay did him no good at all?

If he truly loved Hailey, he'd want what was best for her. Whoa. Love? It had all been lust back in the day. And yet, the feelings had never gone away completely, though they'd definitely morphed. But all the way to love?

He was *not* like the dog in the manger. He wasn't only out to make it difficult for Hailey to move on without him. She'd had twelve years to do that, and so had he. It hadn't worked. Not for him or, by the looks of it, for her.

Did he stand a real chance for a future with her? And the bigger question was, did he even want one after her revelation? Forgiveness was a hard thing, but the Lord only knew he'd done a lot of stuff himself. He'd driven under the influence on more than one occasion. He'd only been caught once, that's all.

He was lucky he'd never caused a fatality. Or maybe it wasn't luck. Maybe God had been looking out for him. At least, that's what Dad said at the time.

Basil had to forgive Hailey. He didn't know how, but it had to happen, whether there was a future for the two of them or not. He couldn't live with himself, couldn't get his life on track, by holding onto the anger and bitterness.

"What are you staring at me for?" Hailey's brows pulled together as she crossed her arms over her chest.

He stepped closer and brushed his thumb over her cheek. "Just a little flour there. I got it."

"There was not." She glowered at him.

"Was, too." An infinitesimal amount, but still. He'd stand by it.

His thumb still tingled from the brief contact. What would she do if he kissed her? Because suddenly he wanted more than that tiny touch. Way more.

"We need to get Ranta Landscaping—" Kass's voice started and stopped abruptly, pulling Basil's attention back to the present.

This was not the time or the place to entertain thoughts of kissing Hailey. Not with her cousin looking quizzically between them. With Uncle Dino soldering water lines and Basil's crew laying recycled-plastic planks not ten feet away.

But soon.

Hailey huffed and turned to Kass. "Linnea had some great ideas for the courtyard down there. Did I forget to show you? A few more tables tucked between the trees. I think the area will clean up nicely."

Kass wrinkled her nose. "We've ignored that space between the bistro and the business building for so long. At least we've kept the trash picked up."

"It'll make a nicer view for Alex's office and the others on this side of that building," agreed Basil. "Linnea's got a good eye for design. I'm sure you'll like what she'll do there."

"I thought you'd feel bad if we didn't plant veggies there."

He shrugged. "Not everything needs to be about edibles. Not much sun gets in there, so shade-loving plants will do best."

Kass laughed. "I like you, Basil. You've changed."

He had? He hadn't known it showed. "Thanks." What did Hailey think of that? But when he turned to check, she'd walked away and was talking to Dino. Huh.

Kass nudged his arm. "Speaking of liking..." She bobbed her eyebrows and poked her chin toward her cousin.

Basil chuckled. "What's not to like? Hailey's a great girl — woman — just like you."

"Nice try at deflection," Kass murmured. "Is there something between you? Because sometimes I think there is."

If Hailey hadn't told her cousin about their history, it wasn't Basil's place to do so. But had she told anyone about the abortion? Received any counseling or support? Or had she been carrying the burden alone for all these years?

He suspected the latter. And then he'd snapped at her in anger.

Way to go, Santoro. How to make things worse.

⌒‿⌒

"I THINK BASIL LIKES YOU." Kass kicked off her sandals just inside Hailey's apartment.

Hailey waved the words away. "Basil likes anything in a skirt." And she'd been wearing more of them this summer than ever before. Coincidence? Probably not.

"He seems different than before the DUI." Kass tugged open the fridge. "Don't you have anything besides ginger ale?"

"No. My roommate left me years ago, so why should I keep stocking her favorite drinks?"

"Ginger ale is loaded with sugar. It's terrible for you."

Sighing, Kass reached for a glass from the cupboard then pushed it against the fridge's water dispenser.

"Why did I hear that in Astrid's voice?" Probably for the same reason those two cases of pop had been in Hailey's fridge for over a month. She'd drank, what, two of them?

"Astrid invades all my decisions these days."

Hailey narrowed her gaze. "And why would that be?"

"I guess you'll be the first to know. Besides Wesley, anyway. I'm pregnant, and when I carried Eleanor, I was borderline gestational diabetic. So, I'm going to need to be careful this time around."

"Wait, what? Eleanor is only fifteen months old." That should not have been the first thing out of her mouth.

Kass drank the whole glass down and turned to refill it. "I can do the math."

"Well, congratulations! I'm happy for you guys." She would be, once she'd had time to adjust. In the meantime, she could put some pep in her voice.

"Thanks. I figured you should know why I've missed so much work lately."

"I'm sorry. It hasn't only been Eleanor not feeling well then?"

Kass shook her head. "This pregnancy is harder than with her. I don't know why, but they do say each is different. I had no idea how true that could be."

Hailey wouldn't likely ever find out. She steeled herself not to react. "So... what's going to happen downstairs? You won't be able to work so many hours with two babies."

"You are full of truth bombs, Lady Obvious. That's why I came over."

Hailey managed a smile. "And here I thought you came

to hang out because I'm your cousin and you missed me or something."

"That, too." Kass took the water glass, plopped into an easy chair, and put her feet on the ottoman.

Hailey followed her into the other room and settled into the corner of the sofa. "Sorry. You caught me by surprise."

"I caught Wesley by surprise, too. Maybe me, too. But I'm pretty excited. You know I always wanted a sister, and having two kids so close in age will be great for them growing up."

"I always wanted a sister, too, and God sent me you."

"Yeah, well, if you were married and having kids right now, then Eleanor might get a cousin playmate like we did, but unless there's something you're not telling me — like you're secretly married and expecting — it falls on me to supply my own child's playmate."

Even seated, Hailey reeled. "I'm definitely not secretly wed or pregnant."

"Yeah, didn't think so." Kass's eyes closed.

At least that meant Kass wasn't analyzing Hailey's facial expressions, which she needed to get back under control this instant.

Except that Kass's lids split slightly. "You know six years ago we talked about both of us getting married and having kids someday and who'd get this apartment when that happened."

Hailey took a deep breath. "Yep, I remember. I guess it's mine by default since you already moved out. But this isn't how I imagined things." Six years ago she'd thought she was over the abortion. Over Basil. Ready to move on with the right guy.

Showed how little she'd known.

"It's not what I expected, either, but I'm so thankful for Wesley rocking me out of my comfort zone. When Adriana told me she'd set you up with a friend of Myles's, I hoped you'd find the same thing."

Hailey snorted. "The guy was a total jerk. Hands-on and lips-on. No thank you."

"You're kidding! That's terrible."

"You're telling me." She shuddered at the memory. "I bailed on the date and walked home from Riverside Park by myself."

"You should have called me."

"It's not far."

"That's not why, silly. Because you needed a friend."

Hailey shrugged. "I was fine." Which wasn't entirely true. "You know, I wouldn't bother even trying to date if I didn't still want a family. I'm thirty, and my childbearing years are speeding by." Not that she deserved pregnancy after how she'd treated the last one. Her singleness was probably God's punishment. Yes, she knew about forgiveness and grace, but face it. That had been a terrible sin.

"Aw, Hailey. I'm sorry. Maybe you should apply to adopt."

What? Hailey reared back and stared at Kass. "Are you crazy? They'd never give a baby to a single person."

"Lenore's niece adopted a baby from Dominican Republic a couple of years ago. It happens."

"Yeah, but my life is so busy. I don't think it's a good idea."

"Well, it's something to think about." Kass grinned. "Or you could marry Basil and add to the Santoro tribe."

"I'm not marrying Basil."

"I think he likes you."

They were back around to this topic, were they? "He's not the sort of guy I'd ever go for." Been there. Done that.

"He's changed."

"So you say. But he's still a player."

"Maybe he's like you, waiting for the right person to come along. You come across as a flirt, you know, but I know that's not the real you."

Her cousin was getting too close for comfort. "I'm not sure why you're fixated on me and Basil."

Kass swung her feet off the ottoman and leaned forward in the easy chair. "Well, you've known him forever. You know his family and that he was raised well. Yes, he's sowed his wild oats, but he's paid for all that. And I sense two things about him."

Hailey raised her eyebrows and waited.

"I sense that he's softer to the things of the Lord. I've seen how he closes his eyes in church and sings softly. The old Basil didn't sing at all. He stood with his arms crossed and feet braced."

Kass had a point there, but Hailey wasn't so sure she wanted to acknowledge it.

"And secondly, I've noticed that his eyes follow you around. When he comes into the bistro, the first thing he does is glance around until he spots you. He sits where he can see into the kitchen. And in a group, he'll look at other people when they're talking or he's talking to them, but in between, he swings back to you."

Hailey laughed. Hopefully it didn't sound as hollow as it seemed to her. "You have a great imagination."

"While that is true, I'm pretty sure I'm not seeing things that aren't there."

"Just no to Basil, okay?"

"Why? Help me understand."

The whole summer in Venice billowed into Hailey's mind like a tangible entity, begging to be put into words, pleading for release to someone she could trust, and who more than her cousin? But there was far too much to be ashamed of in that story. Her wanton behavior. And how it ended.

Tears prickled at Hailey's eyes. She looked down at her hands, clenched in her lap, and shook her head.

"Something happened, didn't it?" Kass asked softly. "Did he try to take advantage of you like Holden did?"

Hailey shook her head some more. Not at all like Holden. Basil hadn't taken advantage of her any more than she had taken advantage of him. Their fling had been totally mutual, the most glorious summer ever, once she'd shoved her conscience into the cellar and rolled a boulder over the trapdoor. But that had all resurfaced when the bliss had faded.

"I wish you felt you could talk to me..."

Hailey inhaled a long breath and forced herself to meet Kass's gaze with a smile. She brushed her hair from her face. "I tell you everything that matters. Now, explain how to keep the bistro running smoothly if you're out of action indefinitely. When's the baby due, anyway?"

11

*H*ey, it's looking good up here." Marco planted both hands on his hips and looked around the project.

Basil rose and shifted his carpentry belt to the side. "Hey, bro. Yeah, Dino's crew finished up a couple of days ago, so we're full-speed ahead on the decking." Which didn't account for why Basil returned most days after the workers had clocked off.

"A couple of weeks to finish?"

"Probably less, though there's always more details in wrap-up than expected."

"How'd you learn to do all this, anyway?"

"YouTube."

Marco rolled his eyes as he loosened his tie. "Seriously."

"Yeah."

"You're kidding, right? Because I can't see Jasmine and Peter turning you loose on a project of this magnitude without hands-on experience to back you up."

"I worked on a couple of projects in Seattle with a

guy who frequented Fireweed. And, yeah, I learned enough from YouTube to get the basics, and he taught me more."

"You had me going for a minute there."

Basil grinned. "Fake it 'til you make it. That's my motto."

"Always was." Marco clapped Basil's shoulder. "Are you happy doing this?"

"As happy as anything."

"That's not exactly an answer."

"Sure, it is." Basil yanked his brother's tie. "Beats working in an office all to pieces."

"I'm not so fond of sweating it out with manual labor."

"Says the guy who's like a grand guru of jiu jitsu."

Marco chuckled. "Grand guru isn't exactly what we call advanced martial artists. But, whatever. Point taken."

"Hey, do you know Holden Latimer?"

"Holden. Holden." Marco scratched his chin. "Yeah, I think so. He comes in for the class after mine with the boys. Friend of Myles Sheridan."

"That's the one. Do you know anything about him?"

"Not really. Why?"

"No reason."

"Oh, sure. That's why you mentioned him in the first place. Because you'd never heard of him and never thought about him."

Busted. "Met him the other day. He took Hailey out."

Marco's eyebrows shot up. "You met him and Hailey on a date?"

"No. I met him at Myles and Adriana's. Then he asked Hailey out. I thought he was kind of sleazy, so I wondered what you thought."

"Hailey's a grownup. I'm pretty sure she could put a guy in his place if needed."

"True."

"Do you have big brotherly feelings toward Hailey? Like she needs you to protect her or something?"

Basil blinked and reared back. "Of course not." Wait, what had he admitted to?

"The other kind of feelings is even more possessive."

"Nah. You're off your rocker, bro."

"Am I?"

Ack, why had Basil opened his mouth? For twelve years, no one in his family or community had suspected a thing. Or, at least, if they had, no one gave any indication. Yeah, he'd been out of town for the past three years. He'd obviously lost his ability to stay aloof.

Was detached really his goal? No. That's why he'd come home, to make amends. He eyed his brother. "Not to change the subject, but I'm going to, anyway. I need to ask you something."

"You just did." Marco smirked.

"No. Seriously. I... I don't think I ever thanked you properly for getting me that job with Public Works after I dropped out of college. You went out on a limb for me, and I didn't show appreciation. But, thank you."

"You're welcome. I know you hated it."

"I did, but that's not the point. The point is you put your reputation on the line for me, and I nearly blew your promotion."

"It worked out. It's okay, Basil."

"I know I've been a lousy brother."

"Don't tell me there's more to this confession." Trust Marco to try and lighten the atmosphere.

"There's always more. I've screwed up in more ways than I can count, but you've always been there for me. Let me hang out with your kids. If you worried about my influence over them, you didn't let on."

"The boys think you're the greatest."

Basil shook his head. "You and I know better. I'll try and be a better role model for them in the future."

"Dude. Where's Basil, and what have you done with my brother?"

"Be serious."

"I'm not used to having this sort of conversation with you."

"I bet you do with Alex and Evan, though."

"Yeah, well, they've always appreciated an older brother's advice."

"Unlike me."

"I just want you to know I've always appreciated you. Concerned about your choices? Yes. But you're a great guy, and I'm proud to be your brother."

"Except for that one night three years ago, maybe..." Basil hunched his shoulders as he jammed his steel-toed boot against the pile of planking.

"I was proud of the way you accepted responsibility and paid your debt to society," Marco responded quietly.

"Jasmine never saw any good in me."

"I think the real problem has been that you never saw any good in yourself."

Nailed it. "Maybe it didn't seem there was any good to see, so why bother?"

"Because you were made in the image of God, bro. *He* sees worth in you. It's why He died for you."

Basil shrugged. "He died for everyone. It's hard to imagine it was anything personal."

"But it was. I remember when you were a kid and gave your life to Jesus."

He remembered, too. He'd been so young. What, seven or eight? But he'd sure believed. He'd felt so forgiven. So loved.

"Then what happened?" Marco asked softly.

"Hormones, I guess. I had something to prove."

"Did it satisfy you?"

Basil snorted. "You know the answer to that. I partied too much. Drank too much. None of it was ever enough." The sex had never been enough, either, but maybe he didn't need to discuss that with his brother. Marco had been the perfect firstborn. Toed the line all through high school and college and made their parents proud with achievements of every kind. Then he'd married his high-school sweetheart, Daria. Basil would hazard a guess they'd both been virgins until that day.

That ship had sailed a long time ago. Hailey hadn't been his first, but she'd certainly meant the most to him. He'd seen forever in her eyes. Considered it himself.

"So, now what? I don't know what's going on between you and God, bro, but I'd venture a guess you're not going to find true satisfaction and purpose until you get that part figured out. I appreciate the apology. I do. But the one you've hurt the most is Jesus. Start there. It'll be worth it."

Basil slung his arm over his brother's shoulder as a roll of thunder crashed over the building. "For an old guy, you make a lot of sense. Now help me get the tools under cover, would you?"

THEY WERE GOING to have to hire someone to manage the bistro side of the business. Hailey and Kass had employed too many college-age girls who didn't want to make Bridgeview Bakery and Bistro their permanent career. They should have been hiring more middle-aged women all along. Women like Astrid.

But Astrid wasn't managerial material, thank the good Lord. Hailey couldn't see working as a team with the opinionated woman. It was a miracle Astrid had worked for them for three years and hadn't permanently offended any of their regular clients with her outspoken anti-sugar propaganda.

Marley Santoro might be a good fit. She was such an extrovert that she loved covering the lunch shift though she and Alex didn't need the money and it cut into her painting time. But... she was young, and one of these days they'd decide to start a family. Hailey couldn't count on Marley and Kass not overlapping with maternity leave.

Ava had been working some over the summer, but rumor had it she'd scored more teaching work for the next school year. Plus, she was dating Seth Donahue. No, Ava's days at the bistro were numbered.

Gabriella was in her third year of college. She'd be looking for a full-time job in her chosen career next year, so they couldn't count on her much longer, either.

Shay was fine with the customers, but she tended to get stressed out when it was busier than usual. Hailey couldn't see Shay in a management role.

And she was back around to Astrid Jansen. And back to rejecting the thought. It was time for a *now hiring* sign in the window and maybe an ad in the Spokesman-Review.

Hiring staff was a pain. Besides, how could she trust her own judgment? She'd thought she could believe in Basil once, to say nothing of her parents. Look where that had gotten her. If she couldn't count on the people who'd been closest to her, then trusting a stranger was a long shot.

Hailey mentally worked her way down the streets in Bridgeview, thinking about who lived in each house. Someone like Winnie would be ideal, but Winnie was baking for Charlie's coffee truck these days.

Would Fran be interested? She'd been running a daycare from her home for several years, but both Tieri and Luca were in school now. If Fran closed her business, she'd leave a lot of families in the lurch. But maybe it would be worth asking her before running ads. Or she might know someone who'd be interested.

Before she could talk herself out of it, Hailey tapped Fran's number in her cell phone.

"Hailey! How are you doing? It seems ages since we've talked."

Guilt bit deep. She and Fran had never been close — the other woman was five or six years older, so they'd never hung out in school. Plus, Basil's cousin was one of those who'd married and had her kids young. They'd had little in common, especially when Hailey was trying to skirt the Santoro clan.

"Hey! It has been a long time. Summer is always busy down at the bakery."

"When isn't it?" Fran laughed. "And I heard you guys are putting in a rooftop patio. That will only add to the appeal."

"We are! Bridgeview Backyards is in charge." That

seemed better than saying it was Basil's project. "But more appeal can be a problem, too."

"How's that?"

"We're so busy already, and it looks like several of the younger staff will be leaving us in the next while."

"Ava? She's picked up a fourth school for teaching music."

"Yes, I figure she'll soon be leaving completely, and I doubt Gabriella will be far behind."

"I'm sure. You guys need to hire some older women."

Bingo. There was Hailey's opening. "We have Astrid, but she really doesn't want more hours than we're already giving her. Do you know anyone who's looking for steady work?"

"Hmm." Fran sounded thoughtful.

"I was even wondering if you might want to come work for us yourself." There. She'd said it out loud.

"Me? But I have the daycare."

"That's true. Is that what you want to keep doing? I know you provide a very helpful service to Bridgeview families."

"Well, it was never my life's dream, if that's what you're asking."

Hailey couldn't help the little jump of joy in her heart.

"I wanted to stay home with the kids, but we couldn't quite afford to live on Tad's income. Watching other people's kids was the perfect solution."

"Luca's in school now, isn't he?"

"He is..."

"Well, if you decide it's time for a change, let me know. Or if you know someone else who might be a good fit."

"Are you thinking of the kitchen or the front end?"

"Mostly the bistro, though it wouldn't hurt for me to have someone else in the kitchen. If any of us are sick, there's no one to pick up the slack. Would cooking and baking be more interesting to you than out front?"

"I'd go crazy." Fran laughed. "The hardest thing with daycare is not having adults around to talk to. I must say, the thought of people around me all day does sound appealing."

"I think you're calling me not-a-people." Hailey laughed, too. "Seriously, I get it. Kass and I have often marveled that I'm stuck in the kitchen while she runs the public side, and she's so much more introverted than I am. Still, it plays to both our strengths in other ways."

"I'm curious why it's you calling instead of Kass if you're looking for serving staff. Like you said, isn't that her department?"

"Sure, but we run the team together. Everything affects both of us."

Kass hadn't said Hailey should keep the pregnancy a secret, but she also hadn't said she could blab it to the neighborhood. There'd be time enough for that later. Then Fran would recall this conversation and understand.

"I was just about to put an ad in the paper since I'm down a couple of families. I only have Gavin full-time, and then Lillian in the mornings."

"I'd hate to be responsible for messing up Dafne's college schedule, or Jasmine's work, for that matter."

"You know, let me think on this for a day or two, and talk it over with Tad. When would you need an answer?"

"Really?" Hailey couldn't keep the hope out of her voice. "I thought it was a total long shot."

"It kind of is." Fran giggled. "But if the hours could line up with the elementary school, it just might work."

"What time is that?"

"The kids are in school eight-thirty to two-forty-five. Tad doesn't start work until nine, so he could get them to school, so long as I was home when they were done. Hmm, I'm starting to like this idea."

"You and Tad talk it over then. I'll still feel guilty for poaching the best babysitter in Bridgeview, but I'll get over it."

Fran laughed. "I'll get back to you in a couple of days."

Hailey tapped to end the call after they'd wound down. Was it a mistake hiring another of the Santoro cousins? It was hard to avoid them, since they made up half the neighborhood. Or at least a quarter. But Fran was the oldest of the crew and already had her family. She wouldn't likely be looking for maternity leave or a better job, at least if Hailey and Kass paid her well.

Maybe Hailey should be looking to hire for the kitchen, too. Was Kass right? Was it possible for a single woman to adopt? Was it sensible or wise?

She'd never been known for wisdom, but she'd be taking on responsibility for another life. It wasn't something she could mess up.

Not again.

12

When Hailey needed to cover the public side, the schedule in the kitchen went out of whack, which soon affected what was available for sale up front. It was a vicious circle, but what was she supposed to do when Kass had been up all night with a teething Eleanor and then spent the morning puking?

It meant Hailey ran back and forth in the two hours their shifts usually overlapped then hung up her chef's hat and took on Kass's usual duties.

Today, that meant she was standing behind the counter pouring coffee and plating goodies when Marietta entered the bistro. The neighborhood matriarch took the whole space in with a sweeping look, her gaze pausing on her granddaughter Gabriella then her granddaughter-in-law Marley before settling on Hailey.

"Good afternoon, Marietta. Can I pour you a coffee?" Hailey offered with a bright smile.

"You are busy."

Half the tables were full even at four o'clock. Groups

of businessmen loosened their ties and talked shop. A few men and women had laptops open, tapping away. Some moms and kids surrounded three tables, catching up now that school was back in session. Chatter and laughter filled the air, smothering the low music they always kept on.

"Coffee and a cinnamon roll if you have any left. I see my sons." Marietta pointed toward the back corner where the Santoro men tended to gather. They'd be in for a shock when their table disappeared to make way for access to the outside stairs.

"We're out of the regular cinnamon rolls, but I have two Keto ones left. Would you like to try one?"

Marietta glowered. "No, that is sacrilege. It is good for Sadie and others, I suppose, but not for me." She pointed into the display case. "Two cookies, if they have real sugar."

"They do. I'll bring them out to you."

Marietta nodded as though she expected nothing less. That might be true, actually. She made her way between the tables, stopping for a minute to chat with the group of moms before carrying on to where Ray, Dino, and Franco sat.

Hailey plated the cookies, poured the coffee, and carried both out to Marietta.

"Hailey!" exclaimed Basil's dad. "We don't often see you on this side of the counter."

"Hi, Ray. Kass stayed home with Eleanor today. Poor baby is teething, and I guess no one got any sleep."

"Kassidy is lucky she has you, but it must make a long day."

"It sure does. I've been here for twelve hours now, with two to go."

Franco nudged out a chair with his foot. "It's quiet for a minute. Sit. Take a load off."

Hailey glanced around, but Franco was right. Did he know his daughter was thinking of working here? It was all Hailey could do after a day like this not to phone Fran and beg for a yes.

She sank into the chair where she could still see if anyone entered. Gabriella could handle things for a few minutes, but Hailey'd be ready to jump up if needed.

Hailey turned to Dino. "Thanks for hooking up the waterlines on the rooftop. It's looking good up there."

"I have not seen this rooftop," Marietta complained.

"It's a lot of stairs, Mamma," Dino said.

"I am not such an old woman." She glared at her son.

"It's not ready for tours yet," Hailey put in hastily. "Last I saw, it was still a mess up there."

Ray leaned back in his chair. "Basil tells me there's another week or so to go. He texted me some photos yesterday." He nodded at Hailey. "I think it will prove to be a popular addition. You'll be even busier."

"I kind of dread that, which I probably shouldn't say out loud."

Basil's dad guffawed. "If you can't tell us, you can't tell anyone. It's true, though. You need more staff, especially if you have to fill in for Kassidy when she's not available."

"It's true." Hailey focused on *not* looking at Francesca's dad. "If you know anyone who's looking for work, send them in. Especially someone who might stay long-term."

Marietta's brows furrowed immediately as though she alone had been tasked with finding the bistro's next employees.

The street door opened, and Hailey immediately started

to rise before she realized it was Basil. A flush shot up her face. Great. All she needed was for him to see her schmoozing with his family, but there was nowhere to hide. He'd seen her, and his characteristic smirk appeared.

"Hey, Gabby, bring me a coffee, will you?" he asked his cousin as he wended toward the Santoro table.

"Sure thing. Don't forget to tip me."

The moms and kids cleared out, and one of the workers packed up his laptop and headed out. Suddenly, the din in the place dropped to less than half.

Maybe Gabby and Marley could handle things until closing. Maybe Hailey could head up to her apartment and collapse. Now, before Basil... but it was too late, of course. He bent and brushed a kiss on Marietta's cheek. "Hi, Nonna."

He pulled out the chair next to Hailey's, whipped it around, and straddled it. At least that kept him from getting too close.

"Good day, Basil. Are you sleeping well? You look tired."

"I'm fine, Nonna." A grin played at the corners of his mouth, which Hailey shouldn't notice. Especially when he caught her looking, and that grin turned into a smirk.

"Young people these days." Marietta flung her hands out. "Not everything needs to be accomplished in one minute. Life is too short. You must also slow down and enjoy it."

Silence fell for a moment. Hailey imagined the men remembering their brother Alberto, Gabby's dad, who'd passed away several years earlier. Life was indeed short... and hard to balance. Didn't a short life mean you should try to pack in everything you could?

Hailey had been doing that, but she'd kept herself so busy that peace and purpose had eluded her.

She cast a sideways glance at Basil only to find him watching her. They'd slowed down and enjoyed things in Venice. It wasn't always the wisest move.

ᕙᶫᶜ

BASIL HADN'T MEANT to hang around Bridgeview Bakery and Bistro for this long, but he also hadn't expected to find Hailey chatting with Nonna and the uncles. Inexplicably, she hadn't darted back to the kitchen upon his arrival, and he certainly wasn't going to walk out as long as she stayed.

Eventually, Nonna rose to her feet, and Uncle Dino leaped up to walk out with her. A few minutes later, Dad and Uncle Franco wandered out, still deep in conversation about last Sunday's sermon.

Hailey jumped up. "Oh my. It's nearly five. I have to—"

Basil's hand caught on her forearm. "Why is it your duty?"

"Because Kass had to take the day off. I should never have sat so long."

"Looks like Marley and Gabby have got it."

Only two other customers remained. Gabby wiped out the display case, though it wasn't quite closing time. "But—"

He pressed lightly on her arm. "Talk to me."

Hailey sank back into her chair, but her eyes narrowed at him. "Is everything okay with the project?"

"Yes."

"Then we have nothing to talk about."

"Wrong."

Her eyebrows peaked.

Here went nothing. "I'm sorry I got so angry with you the other day."

Fire flared in her eyes then doused as though by a bucket of water. "I deserved it."

"You didn't. It happened a long time ago, and I need to forgive you and move on. But that means I need to ask you to forgive me for my part, too."

Hailey's gaze swept the bistro quickly, but he'd kept his voice low, and there was no one near enough to overhear. "It was both of us."

"I forgive you. Do you forgive me?" Basil held his breath.

"Of course." She started to rise.

Again, he caught her arm. "Hailey, don't run. Please. Because then I don't feel like you're ready to move on."

"There is no moving on."

"There could be." He wanted to slide his hand up her arm, but his cousins were in the room, so he pulled back. They might not be able to overhear, but they sure wouldn't miss a lingering touch.

"Basil, you know better. There is no you and me."

"There could be," he repeated. "There's never been anyone else for me, Hailey. Not like you."

She darted a glance at him then looked down at her hands clenched in her lap. "Right. The other hundred women you slept with meant nothing."

He winced. "I know that sounds unlikely, but it's still true. I wasn't just running from you. I was running from God."

"Are you still?" A note of wistfulness crept into her voice.

Basil let out a long breath. "I'm working through it. I've got a lot of selfish thinking to get rid of. It's been a long time since I tried to put God first." He hesitated then plunged ahead. "How are things with you and God?"

"Mostly a habit." She swallowed hard. "It's not that I don't believe. I do. It's..."

"It's that there's a barrier," he finished for her.

"Yeah." This time she met his gaze for more than half a second before looking away.

"We could try to find our way back together."

Hailey closed her eyes. "I don't think that's a good idea, Basil."

"I think it is. Because I'm willing to guess you don't have anyone else you've told all this to. I know I haven't."

"You're right. I haven't. But—"

Basil dared to touch her shoulder again, when what he really wanted to do was cup her face and kiss her. Whoa. This was not the time or place. Besides, this conversation wasn't about them as a couple. It was about healing from their mutual past. About both of them finding a footing in their faith once again.

But it could lead to a future together, couldn't it? Was it so wrong to hope for that?

He shook his head. Who'd ever have thought that perpetual cynic Basil Santoro was finally serious about faith and love? But he was. He definitely was.

"See? Even you know it's a bad idea."

What? Oh. She'd caught his head shake. "It's the best idea I've had in twelve years. I should have treated you with respect that summer in Venice, Hailey. You were never my personal plaything, just there for a temporary fling."

"It was both of us," she whispered.

"It was. But I was still wrong, and I'm sorry. And I'm super sorry I wasn't around for the aftermath. That I didn't even know what was going on. You had a lot to deal with on your own. I can't tell you how much I regret that."

"My parents are coming for a visit soon."

Basil blinked at the change of topic, but quickly realized the link. "You don't see much of them."

Hailey shook her head. "I hated them as much as I hated you. And they seemed content to let me go my own way after that."

"When are they coming, and how long are they staying?"

"In just a couple of weeks, but I don't know for how long." She sighed. "Even overnight is too long."

"Maybe they're here to mend the relationship."

"I doubt it."

"Hey, you two gonna sit here and talk all night? I'm ready to lock the front door."

Basil glanced at Marley. When had she come near, and what had she overheard? "I've got a key to the backdoor, so go ahead."

His sister-in-law raised her eyebrows at him.

"To access the roof via the back stairs," he clarified. "I work up there, remember?"

"Right." She looked between him and Hailey.

Hailey surged to her feet. "I need to go. Thanks for wrapping things up, Marley. Is Gabby still here?"

"Yes, she's cleaning the restrooms."

"I'll go check on her. Go ahead and lock up on your way out, Marley."

"Okaaay." With another dubious look, she made her way out the door and locked it.

"Sorry." Basil stood beside Hailey. "I didn't mean to raise eyebrows in your staff."

"Half my staff is related to you."

He laughed. "I can't help that. You hired them."

"They're great girls, but I sure don't need them mulling over our relationship."

"Oh, now we have a relationship? I'll take it."

"You're insufferable."

"So they say." Basil looked out the windows to see Marley disappearing up the sidewalk. Gabriella must still be in the back. He reached for Hailey's hand and gave it a squeeze, shielding the movement from the kitchen entrance, just in case. "Give me a chance, Hailey? Please?"

This time she studied his face for a long moment. "I'm going to regret this."

His heart leaped. "You're agreeing!"

"I already regret it."

"But you won't back out, because you don't retreat from a challenge. You don't know how."

"Basil, I don't know how to do this, either. And I truly think it's a bad idea. It's just... it's been so long. I feel so alone. So... wicked. And I don't know where to go from here."

Like he was honestly able to help her? He didn't know, either. But together they could find a way.

"Go for dinner with me?" he asked impulsively.

"Bad idea. I don't want to be seen with you, and I'm exhausted."

"You're too tired to cook, and you need to eat."

"You're not welcome in my apartment, and I don't want to go to yours."

"That's fair. Meet me at Morley's in half an hour? It's far

enough out of Bridgeview it's unlikely we'll run into anyone we know."

"Mmm. They make the best burgers and cheesecake."

Basil pumped his fist. "I win!"

"Juvenile." But she was smiling.

And somehow, against all odds, he had a date with the woman who'd never left his thoughts.

13

*I*n the few minutes it took Hailey to touch up her makeup, change her clothes, and drive across the bridge to Morley's, she talked herself out of bailing at least five times.

What on earth was she doing, agreeing to meet Basil? She would *not* call this a date, because a date could lead to another one... could lead to a future. She and Basil had no future. What they had was a past that needed to be firmly dealt with, once and for all.

They could have done that without dinner. They'd pretty much done it in the corner of the bistro before Marley reminded them it was closing time and eyed them speculatively.

She should have refused, but the diner's burgers were some of the best in Spokane, and she didn't bother going often enough. It was no fun by herself. It wasn't going to be fun with Basil, either.

His truck was already parked along the street when she drove up. Hailey took a deep breath as she parked behind him and exited her car. Bad idea. Really bad idea. But she walked in anyway, smiled at the hostess, and slid into the booth across from Basil.

"Hey." His blue eyes took her in. "You look better already. It must be the company."

"It's the thought of dinner I didn't have to scrounge."

"Or buy."

"I can get my own. It's not like this is a date."

He grinned and bobbed his eyebrows. "It could be."

Hailey was starting to have trouble remembering why it shouldn't be. They were both older now. Wiser, hopefully.

"What can I get you?" The young server stood beside their table, pen poised over an order pad.

Basil rattled off their order. He'd recalled what she liked, which ought to feel creepy. Instead, it made Hailey feel remembered. Cared for.

When their drinks arrived, Hailey wrapped both hands around her chilled glass of ginger ale and studied it. Better than looking at Basil. What if he read the indecision — the potential capitulation — in her face?

He stretched his legs under the table, his foot bumping hers. He didn't apologize, and he didn't move away. Instead, his sandal gently tapped the side of hers.

The man was very hard to ignore. He'd practiced for years. On other women, not just her. But he'd said that was over, that no one had meant as much to him as she had. Could she believe him? She peeked at him through her lashes and caught him watching her.

He grinned.

Drat him for being so observant. And what was to be gained by pretending she hadn't met him on purpose? Nothing. It would be better to face him fully and make him realize they couldn't move on together. First, she needed to convince herself.

"Do you think we need counseling?" he asked quietly.

"I... what?"

"Counseling. You know, someone wise to talk to who can help us deal with the past."

"I don't want to talk about it with anyone else."

"You haven't told anyone." It was a statement, not a question.

"Not since my parents. Then you."

"So, I can tell my parents."

Hailey's gaze flew to meet his. "No."

"But yours know, so it would only be fair."

And have Ray and Grace look down on her for leading their son astray? But it wouldn't be for that. It would be for murdering their grandchild. Tears welled in her eyes. "No."

"Hailey." Basil reached across the table, loosened her grip from around the glass, and held both her hands.

For a second, she pulled against his grip, but he didn't let go, and she found his warmth and strength comforting. "Basil, I'm so, so sorry."

"I know. I am, too." He hesitated. "But I think if we lock this away, we'll never deal with it. And then I'm not sure we can move forward."

"I don't deserve to move forward." Whether he meant together or alone, she didn't know. But either way, she wasn't worthy.

"You do."

This time she pulled her hands from his. "You didn't do it. I did."

"My dad said something to me the other day."

Her gaze flew to meet his again. "You didn't tell him—"

Basil shook his head. "No. It was about me. I've been arrogant and rebellious. I don't need to tell you that. You've seen it. He said God had already forgiven me, and you know what my thought was, right? How could God forgive me when I couldn't even forgive myself?"

Oh, she knew. She and Basil were more alike than she'd care to admit.

"I'm not there yet," Basil admitted, trapping her gaze. "But when I look at you and see what you've been through, my dad's words make sense. And if they make sense for you, they have to make sense for me."

Hailey tried to wrap her brain around that. Did she believe God forgave when asked? Of course, she did. What kind of Christian would she be if she didn't accept such a basic biblical truth? God had forgiven Dafne for her teen rebellion. Forgiven Dixie for running from Him with all her might, for sleeping with a bunch of guys and having babies with three of them before letting God — and Dan — capture her. God had forgiven Kass's husband, Wesley, for the life he'd led before finding Jesus, too.

But was that the key? Except for Daf, who'd only been a kid, they hadn't been believers. Hailey had. She'd willfully tossed her relationship with God out the window in Venice. No one would ever find out what happened that summer... and that had been true for twelve years. Now Basil knew. And he thought she should go public.

Well, maybe he didn't mean to announce it from the pulpit of Bridgeview Bible Church or put an ad in the Spokesman-Review, but if his parents knew, wouldn't his siblings find out? And Marietta. Basil's grandmother already seemed to have judged Hailey and found her lacking.

The clink of plates on the end of the table interrupted

Hailey's thoughts. Basil reached for her hand, bowed his head, and said a short grace as though he'd been talking to God his entire life.

Hailey froze in shock, unable to gather her thoughts enough to yank her hand away before he said amen. She hadn't even closed her eyes, just stared at him with her mouth hanging open.

He offered a lopsided grin then poked his chin toward her plate. "Enjoy."

BASIL KEPT the conversation to small talk while they enjoyed their burgers and fries. He over-ruled Hailey's minor protest at ordering two slices of cheesecake, but she was the one who'd brought up the diner's signature dessert earlier, so he knew she wanted some. Now he held the door for Hailey as they exited Morley's.

She pressed a hand over her stomach. "I'm sooo stuffed."

He laughed. "Me, too. I may know how to cook, but it's not that fun cooking for one."

"Tell me," she groaned.

Basil bumped her with his elbow. "I just did."

For half a second, it seemed she leaned against him. Just long enough to set his pulse racing and send his reluctance at going straight to his empty apartment surging. "Want to walk? There's a park nearby."

"Ack, I need to wear off a few of these calories."

That was affirmative. Basil threaded his fingers with hers and pulled her toward the sidewalk.

To his surprise, Hailey didn't snatch her hand away.

Why did it matter so much to him? It wasn't like he'd returned to Spokane with the goal of making up with her. They'd had years to do that already and had managed to slide through by rarely speaking to each other.

But maybe Hailey *was* why he'd returned. The stated reason had been to make amends for his past, and who deserved that more than the woman beside him?

The park was only a couple of city blocks in size with a playground at one end and a few trees and a small pond over the remainder. A path encircled the area. A group of kids clambered on the jungle gym while moms chatted on park benches nearby, but no one seemed to be taking in the pond.

A dozen times Basil stopped himself from pressing Hailey more about their shared past. It was difficult to remember there were other topics. They'd walked the loop twice, hand in hand, before he finally thought of something to say. "What are your hopes for the future?"

Her fingers convulsed in his, but he didn't let go.

"I've always wanted to have a family." Her voice broke.

"Oh, honey." He pulled her into his arms, and she cried into his chest until his shirt was soaked. He ran his hands up and down her back until she finally pulled away slightly. "I'd offer you a hanky if I had one, but I'm not the kind of guy who carries one around."

She gave him a watery smile. "No one does anymore."

"Here's my shirt-tail, though." He undid the bottom couple of buttons and offered her the hem.

Hailey shook her head, laughing. "It's okay." She wiped below her eyes with her fingertips. "Sorry for blubbering all over you."

"My privilege." And he meant it. He laced his fingers

with hers again and tugged her back to walking, though his arms felt cold and empty without her wrapped in them. "I want a family, too. I've always kind of envied Marco."

"Marco?" Hailey repeated incredulously.

"Yeah. You know, my brother. The one who married his high-school sweetheart who then popped out three little boys, each more of a handful than the last. *That* Marco."

"I never dreamed you really wanted kids."

Basil bit hard on his bottom lip before he could ask if that was why. It wasn't. It was because her parents had pressured her, but if he'd been there, if he'd been around and supportive, maybe her decision would have been different. This fell firmly in the can't-redo-the-past camp.

He swung her hand. "I've been hard to read."

"You have. Maybe I have, too."

Basil glanced at her. "How so?"

"I've pretended not to envy Kass and Wesley. She's such a great stepmom to Sebastian and mom to little Eleanor. And they're going to have another." She clapped her free hand over her mouth. "Oops. Forget you heard that. They're not telling people yet."

"And all the while, you can't forget what happened in Italy." He kept his voice quiet and as neutral as possible.

"Yeah." She sniffled. "Kass said I should apply to adopt a baby. Her stepmom's niece is single, and she adopted from Dominican Republic."

Or Hailey could marry him, and they'd have their own. Or adopt together. Whichever.

An adrenaline spike accompanied the thought blasting through him, and he nearly reeled. When he'd planned to ask Hailey's forgiveness, he'd never expected his long-dormant emotions would shoot every which direction like fireworks on a short fuse.

Basil tamped down the plethora of feels and kept his voice casual. "Sounds like an interesting idea. Parenting is a lot of work for a person alone. My mom always said there was a reason God gave kids two parents. They needed each other to punt responsibility and activities to."

"My parents punted me to my grandparents. Apparently, it took two people to create me and two others to raise me. I didn't think I was that difficult."

He squeezed her fingers and was rewarded by a firm grip in return. "I can't imagine that amount of disconnect. My parents loved me. There was never any doubt. They just didn't quite know how to cope with me after perfect Marco. And then they had Jasmine, so they probably wondered where I'd really come from."

Her shoulder pressed into his arm. "Don't say that. Your parents are amazing. I know they loved you. Still do."

The contact and the word love distracted him and sent those emotions into a spiral once again. When she didn't shift away from him instantly, he let go of her hand and slipped his arm around her waist. They walked a few more steps, slightly out of synch and bumping awkwardly, before she returned the gesture.

Her trust was fragile. He knew it. There were a thousand ways this could go wrong, some of them in the next two minutes. And yet... Basil couldn't help the hope surging through him.

Maybe, just maybe, he and Hailey could overcome the past between them and find their footing together. It was high time.

If only he didn't know himself so well. He'd screwed up

every good thing that had ever happened to him. Why should this be any different?

If there was ever a time or a reason to get on his knees before God, this was it. It was the only thing he could think of that had any hope of preserving this delicate balance.

14

---

*H*ailey let herself into the building, thankful for the motion sensor lights in the stairwell as she climbed to her apartment. She couldn't believe how many times she and Basil had circled that park, not that she'd kept count.

After she'd cried all over him, they'd walked and walked, talking about everything and nothing. Everything except Venice, but they'd covered that already.

She unlocked her door and froze in the doorway. "Kass? What are you doing here?"

"Waiting for you. I was about to give up, though. Where were you?"

Hailey turned and hung her clutch from a hook behind the door. "Ever heard of a phone call?"

"Ever heard of leaving your phone turned on?"

Oops. Guilty. After Basil had ignored a call from his brother, they'd both set their cells to silent. Not that Hailey needed to explain anything to her cousin. "I was busy and forgot to turn it back on."

"Busy doing what?" Kass lay draped over the easy chair, knees over one padded arm. Didn't look like she'd be heading out any minute soon.

And all Hailey wanted to do was savor the memories of this evening. Relive the conversation and the sensations evoked by being held in Basil's arms.

Hailey smoothed her long top over her hips and studied Kass. "Is everything okay? After the night and morning you had, I'd expect you to be in bed early."

"Eleanor is still rough. Wesley told me to take some time for myself, and the first place I thought of was here."

"Wesley's a good daddy."

"He's the best. But where were you?"

Hailey wasn't given to lying, but she really didn't want to have this conversation with Kass tonight. Maybe not ever. "I decided to go out for dinner. A Morley's burger called my name."

"You don't like eating out by yourself."

"This is true." Hailey angled into the kitchen. "Want a ginger ale?"

"No. I'm supposed to cut sugar, remember?"

Right. The gestational diabetes thing. "Water?" Probably a better idea for her, too. She'd had two glasses of pop at the diner, so she was probably already buzzing. Nah, she was buzzing from Basil.

"No, thanks. I already had some."

"Okay." Hailey filled a glass and turned back to find Kass still studying her.

"So, you either stayed out by yourself for a very long time, or you went with someone."

Hailey took a long drink of water.

"Gabby said you and Basil sat and talked for over half an

hour after closing, until she was putting the chairs upside down to mop the floors."

"Sounds like Gabby is living up to her name."

"So... it's true? You keep telling me you don't like Basil, but the evidence seems to indicate otherwise."

"We did sit and talk."

"And then went to Morley's together?"

"Jeepers, woman. I didn't know you'd been FBI in a former life."

"I must have nailed it." Kass surged into an upright sitting position and began chanting, "Hailey and Basil sitting in a tree, k-i-s-s—"

"You've got it wrong. There was definitely no kissing." She'd kind of wished there had been, but it was too early. Far too early... and possibly too late.

Kass waved her hand in dismissal. "It's wise to leave that for the second date. Or maybe you've been going out for the past few weeks, and this is just the first I've heard of it?"

"We have not been going out."

"Spill the deets."

Basil thought they shouldn't guard their history as closely as they had been, but Hailey was not ready to talk about Venice, let alone the baby. Not to Kass. Not to anyone.

"There's not much to tell. I've known him forever. I hung around with Jasmine all through school. Her parents' house was open to all their kids' friends, so I knew Jasmine's four pesky brothers. And we've gone to the same church our whole lives, too."

"Yeah, but when did you *notice* him?"

"Oh, I had a little crush on him back then. You know

how it is when your best friend has a cute big brother. No big deal." Not until Venice. Then it had exploded.

"Um." Kass eyed her. "There still seems to be a big gap between a teenage crush and suddenly, randomly, going out when you're thirty."

"This is really why you came over? To give me the third degree? Can't a woman and a man be friends and enjoy dinner together without it meaning anything?"

"Uh uh. Not when it's you and Basil."

Hailey forced herself to drop into the other chair and act relaxed. "Why did Gabby phone you, anyway? Did she have a problem with closing up tonight?" That couldn't be it. Gabriella had been their closer for a couple of years.

"She wanted to make sure I'd ordered more creamers on our dairy order. And to tattle on you."

"Bridgeview," Hailey muttered.

"I know, right? It's hard to keep a secret around here. But no one has guessed about my pregnancy yet, so thank you for that." A soft smile crossed Kass's face. "Wesley is over the moon."

"That's great. I'm happy for you both." It was hard infusing excitement into those words, but Hailey did her best. "But if there's nothing else, don't mind me if I fall asleep right here. Three-thirty comes mighty early. Do you think you'll be in tomorrow?"

"I certainly plan to." Kass stood and stretched. "You know you can tell me anything, right?"

"I know."

Kass sighed as though she realized that wasn't the magic opening to get Hailey to spill. "Okay, I'm going."

"Want me to walk you home?"

"Nah. Then I'd just have to walk you back. Thanks, though."

"Anytime. Call me when you get there."

The door finally closed behind Kass.

Hailey listened until she heard the heavy metal door downstairs clink shut then she collapsed onto the sofa and closed her eyes. Maybe she could still conjure up all the feels from the amazing hours with Basil.

But that was probably a mistake, just like the whole evening had been. She should have held her ground instead of letting him sweet-talk her. She'd cried all over the front of him! He'd let her — held her sweetly — but she needed to get a grip. That couldn't happen again.

Hadn't she learned anything in her sordid life? She couldn't trust anyone but herself, and even that was dubious.

How about God? She knew the answer to that. Of course, she could trust her Heavenly Father. But He somehow still kept His distance, sort of like her own dad did. Fathers weren't all they were cracked up to be.

Hers was coming to visit. He might not have had a part in pushing for the abortion, but he'd known. He'd left the discussion to her mother.

Hailey should have argued. Should have come home without complying. She hadn't been a child anymore, but she still hadn't wanted to cause problems for her parents. If she'd expected they would love her more for her capitulation, she should have known better. They'd never really loved her. They'd never wanted her. She'd been an accident and should be thankful *she* hadn't been terminated.

Tears trickled down her cheeks, and she let them fall. This wasn't as therapeutic as her earlier tears. There was no one to hold her now. She should be used to it, though Grandma had tried to fill the gap.

She couldn't trust Basil to stick around, either. He hadn't before. Why would he now? No one did.

Hailey imagined wrapping up this beautiful evening in a package with a pretty bow. She stuffed the mental picture in a lockbox and threw it in the ocean then flung the key into a volcano. Mount St. Helens would do.

No more being vulnerable.

BASIL STOOD to one side as Jasmine and Peter prowled around the rooftop.

"This is great!" Peter shook his head as though he couldn't believe that Basil had anything to do with the transformation.

Jasmine turned on a tap and shut if off again. "I'm impressed."

Basil pumped his fist.

"Juvenile." But his sister was laughing, so it was okay. "What do Hailey and Kass think?"

He'd like to know the answer to that himself. He'd waited a couple of days to contact Hailey after their date to Morley's — he didn't want to pressure her, and the whole thing felt so fragile. Maybe he shouldn't have waited, since she hadn't picked up a call in the two days since. Had he missed his window of opportunity?

"As far as I know, they'll be coming up top shortly." He checked his watch. "I'm not sure if either have been sneaking peeks lately. Zeke, Dino, and Franco will be coming on the weekend to cut the opening from the bistro to the stairwell, and then we've got a few finishing touches to wrap up before they open up again on Tuesday."

"It's like you thought of everything." Peter clapped him on the shoulder.

"I tried." Basil might be playing it cool, but his team's approval meant everything to him. Almost everything. Hailey's would mean the most, and it wasn't just because she and Kass were the ones cutting the final check. He wanted to please her.

The mechanical area was hidden behind a lattice wall on the south side overlooking the alley, as well as the inside stairs and a small kitchen with a fridge and a coffee station. He'd even installed a dumbwaiter to the kitchen so staff could easily serve patrons without having to run two long flights of stairs.

Garden beds — empty save a few late-season flowers he'd found languishing at a garden center — dotted the area, equipped with automatic waterers. Some tables were shaded by retractable screens while others — those on the side overlooking the river — were rigged with large umbrellas. Plexiglass rimmed with bands of steel rails rounded the perimeter of the flat roof.

It looked pretty darn good, if he did say so himself.

But all that faded away as Hailey and Kass entered the space from the kitchenette. Kass stopped in midstep and grabbed Hailey's arm. "Oh, my goodness! This is so much better than I envisioned!"

The only reaction Basil was looking for was Hailey's. She looked around with a smile and a nod, but he was distracted by the cute turquoise sundress she was wearing. He'd seen it on her before, and he loved the look on her. He might even have told her. Was that why she'd worn it today?

Probably not, or she'd have replied to the texts he'd sent. She'd obviously seen them, or she wouldn't have come up top right now.

Mixed messages, his Hailey. Only he wasn't sure if she was really his.

Jasmine grabbed Hailey's hands. "Isn't it amazing? My brother is a genius!"

Hailey laughed and hugged Jasmine, turning them toward the view... away from Basil. "It's great. I think our clients will love having their coffee up here."

"And everything will be ready by Tuesday morning?" asked Kass.

Basil tore his gaze from Hailey and turned to her cousin. "I don't see any reason why not. You're closing early Saturday, right?"

She nodded. "Two o'clock, as requested. I can't tell you how excited the staff is to get a shorter workday."

He laughed. "Zeke will be in place, ready to cut the openings. He and my uncles figure on having the door to the stairwell and the French doors to the side patio installed before they leave on Saturday night. Then Sunday and Monday for trim work and cleanup."

Kass clasped her hands in front of her. "I'm super excited."

"Well, we're almost done. I think Peter figures on planting some fall crops in these beds." Basil stepped aside and gestured to his cousin.

Peter nodded. "Spinach, peas, lettuce... even another round of radishes and carrots. There are quite a few vegetables that will do well in the cooler weather over the next few months before the snow flies."

Basil glanced over to where Hailey and Jasmine peered

into the side yard. Should he insert himself in their conversation or not? Meh. He'd never been undecided before. Why should he start caring now if he was wanted or not?

Those mixed messages from Hailey were messing him up, but he needed to just grab the bull by the horns and act his usual charming self. "Excuse me." He nodded to Kass and Peter then crossed the space and slung an arm over Hailey's shoulders. "Hey, I did good, didn't I?"

She stepped out from under his arm, shaking her head and not meeting his gaze. "It looks terrific. Thank you."

"Just doing my job." Not knowing what to do with his hands following that rejection — though what had he actually expected? — he shoved them into his pockets. "A job I seem to be pretty good at."

His sister laughed. "Ever the humble one. I'm scared to tell you how awesome this is for fear it will go to your head and you'll be insufferable for decades to come. We know how it gets, right, Hailey?"

"Yup. Pompous all the way." Hailey smirked in his general direction but didn't meet his gaze.

His imagination had been all too correct. She hadn't just been busy. Something was wrong. Basil had screwed up again.

Kass called something to Jasmine, who strode back to the others. Hailey started to follow her.

"Hailey." He kept his voice quiet.

"Hey." Still no eye contact, but at least she paused.

"You okay?"

"Sure. Why wouldn't I be?"

"No reason. So... are *we* okay?"

Her gaze flitted to his face then away. "There is no we, Basil."

"There was the other day. Or at least the hope of one."

She shook her head. "I'm sorry I cried all over you, and I'm even more sorry if I led you on. I can't do this." And she walked away.

Taking Basil's heart with her.

15

*A*ren't you going to have disappointed staff members?" Fran asked. "I mean, one of them might be hoping for a promotion."

Hailey shook her head. "We've examined that route, for sure. But there's no one ready to step up."

Kass leaned on the table. "Shay would be the closest, but she doesn't want the responsibility."

"You're scaring me." Fran laughed, but not entirely freely. "Is there that much to learn?"

"This is Kass's department, so I'll let her answer." Hailey tipped her head toward her cousin.

Kass glanced around the bistro before leaning close between them and lowering her voice. "This goes no further at the moment, please, but I'm pregnant. I wasn't half this sick with Eleanor, and a lot of days I can barely function. It's not fair to Hailey or the rest of our staff when I can't make it in... or do my job when I get here. We really need someone totally trustworthy who can manage the public side of our business."

Fran managed to squeal almost completely silently. "Congratulations! That's great. Except for the being horribly sick part."

"Thanks. I'm not as excited as I was a couple of weeks ago, but we'll get through. I just hate how it's affecting this place." Kass gestured to the bustle behind her.

"Makes sense. I talked to Dafne and to Jasmine, and both of them can easily arrange other care for their little ones. So, I think I'd like the challenge here. I've missed being around adults, and Tad is all for the change, as well."

Hailey nearly sagged in relief. "That's terrific. You were both Kass's and my first choice when we began talking about possibilities."

"When can you start?" Kass studied Fran's face.

"When do you need me? Jasmine and Dafne can both pivot within a day or two. Is Thursday okay?"

Kass grimaced. "I think I can survive until then."

"And hopefully a bit longer." Hailey studied her cousin from the corner of her eye. "She needs training, too."

"Right. I keep thinking I should be over the worst of it, but the first trimester isn't nearly over. I'm not due until late March."

"Oh, I was so sick with Luca. I can sympathize."

Hailey glanced at her watch. "I need to get back to work shortly. Is there anything else we need to wrap up?" Because what she didn't need was listening to two mothers compare pregnancy stories.

"Right. White pants or skirt and a white top, as I'm sure you know. We provide the aprons. Hair will need to go in one of these sexy nets. Make sure you have super comfy shoes, because it's a long time to be on your feet, especially when you're not used to it."

"We're open seven to five, which I'm also sure you know," Hailey added. "Shay comes in at six to prep then works until two. Gabby does a split shift — at least until college starts — covering morning and afternoon coffee and clean-up after closing. Marley and Astrid both start at eleven. Kass usually works ten to six, but we already know that won't work for you. I think we'd agreed on eight to three?"

Kass turned to Hailey. "I forgot to tell you Gabby doesn't have afternoon classes this semester, so she's going to keep doing the closing shift for the time being."

"Oh, good." Fran nodded. "I just don't see being able to work that late, not while my kids are still at Bridgeview Elementary, anyway. I don't know how you do it with Sebastian, Kass."

"Wesley's schedule is flexible. Also, remember I facilitate that once-a-month cooking club at the community center. Without all those meals in my freezer, it would make everything so much harder."

"Oh, great idea. I should probably start doing something like that myself. While running the daycare from home, I could manage more easily. I'm going to have to get organized."

Yeah, for Hailey dinner was usually seeing what was left over from the bistro and taking a serving upstairs. She really should be doing a better job herself of making sure she got in enough variety... and veggies. She was often rather low on those. But who wanted to cook for one person? Not her.

"Hey, ladies." Basil's voice came from just above her head, which must mean that was his hand resting on the back of her chair, just touching her shoulder blade. Warming it.

She leaned slightly forward and glanced up. "Basil."

"Hey, cuz." Fran bounced out of her chair and came around to hug him. "It seems I hardly ever see you."

"Yeah, Bridgeview Backyards is keeping me pretty busy. I just needed to consult with Hailey and Kass about cutting the opening to the outside staircase this weekend."

Hadn't they consulted this thing to death already?

Fran beamed at him, rocking on her toes. "That's so great. I've heard good things about the project. Maybe I'll even get to serve up there, because I'm coming to work here!"

"Good for you." Basil glanced at Hailey. "We can talk later if you're busy now."

"She's always busy." Kass laughed. "Better catch her when you've got her."

Hailey's brain froze. Kass didn't know. Did she?

"If you've got a minute?"

"Sure." Hailey gritted her teeth as she pointed at the chair beside Fran, across the table. "Talk fast, because I thought we'd covered everything."

Fran and Basil sat, and Basil leaned over the table, focused on Hailey. "Zeke will be in and out quite a lot, measuring, drilling pilot holes."

"Uh huh."

Kass's elbow touched Hailey's ribs. "Anything else?"

"We'll tape off this back eight feet or so with vapor barrier to keep the dust at a minimum in the rest of the dining room."

"You mentioned that." Kass gestured. "We'll stack the tables and chairs before the girls leave."

Basil glanced at Kass then focused back on Hailey. Whatever he said next was lost on her. What was he trying to do, let everyone know he had a thing for her? Or maybe it looked like Basil's normal level of flirting.

If so, Hailey felt for the other women he'd dallied with. Did each of them get the feeling they were his one-and-only? His forever love? Or was it just her, because of their history? Oh, he had a history with other women, too. She wasn't stupid enough to believe otherwise. Just because her own flirting had been innocent all the years since Venice didn't mean he was the same. He'd had Dixie in the car with him when he ran a police barricade drunk, for goodness' sake. That was way beyond flirting.

"Right, Hailey?" asked Kass.

She blinked. "Pardon me? My mind was elsewhere." She checked the time and pushed back from the table. "I really need to get back in the kitchen. We've got bread coming out of the ovens shortly."

All she saw as she fled was Basil's smirk.

⌒‿‿

HAILEY COULD RUN FROM HIM, but she wasn't actually going anywhere. She and her cousin owned an established business and had just invested a considerable sum of money into expanding to the rooftop and side yard.

Basil could take his time... but he didn't care to, not now that he knew what — who — he really wanted. He needed advice, but no one could give it to him without knowing the whole story, which Hailey didn't want to be made public.

For the next few days, he worked picking produce with Jasmine and Peter — it wasn't like he could confide in either of them — and packed boxes for their CSA subscribers.

The community-supported-agriculture business had expanded, and this was the busiest time of year.

But he still had plenty of nervous energy, so he rode his bike for long, punishing hours every evening he couldn't convince his brothers or cousins to shoot hoops.

Tonight, though, Basil dribbled, faked around Alex, jumped, and shot. Swish. Another basket.

"You're on a roll." Laughing, his brother caught the rebound.

"You're soft from sitting in an office all day." Basil snatched the ball from Alex, but his next shot was blocked.

Alex ducked past him and scored.

"Whatever. You're just lucky."

"Ha." Alex kept control of the basketball, making Basil work for it. "I happen to like owning my own business. But thanks for improving the view out my windows with that reno of the bakery's side yard."

After a few years working for an accountant downtown, Alex and a friend had started their own office a couple of years ago now. But then, Alex had always been the responsible one, buying his house when he was only twenty-four and renting out rooms to help fund the mortgage payments. Now that he was married, he only leased out the basement suite.

Basil sighed, stole the ball back, and sank a basket. He'd lost track of the score a while back. Winning wasn't the point. Hanging out with Alex was. Not thinking about Hailey was.

"Logan and Linnea are buying a house. You want to rent our basement suite?"

"As if." About the last thing he wanted was to hear Alex and Marley overhead. At least Bridgeview Manor had decent barriers between floors. Basil could rarely hear Brittany or Gabriella upstairs.

"Thought I'd give you first dibs." Alex dodged around him, but Basil got his hands on the ball.

"You don't need to do me any favors."

Alex blocked Basil's shot then sank one of his own. "Noted."

"Hey."

"I was going easy on you. Respecting my elders and all that." Alex smirked.

"Sure. That was a fluke." Basil redoubled his efforts, but it seemed Alex had been telling the truth, because the kid scored a few more points in quick succession. No way was Basil calling the game, though.

Finally, Alex bounce-passed the ball and strode toward the picnic table beside the court. "I promised Marley I wouldn't be too long."

"Wouldn't want the little woman getting jealous."

Alex took a long gulp from his water bottle and eyed Basil. "If anyone's jealous, it's you. Married life is good. You should settle down and try it."

The old flippant response nearly leaped from Basil's mouth, but he was trying to do better. Trying to be honest but polite. "Maybe someday." He parked the basketball on the table and pulled out his own water. "Gotta meet the right woman first."

"We have friends. I could set you up..."

"Nope." Memories of watching Hailey and Holden meeting for the first time shot into Basil's mind. "Too many ways that could go wrong."

Alex leaned against the picnic table. "Maybe you've already met her."

No lying, remember? Basil shrugged. "If I have, God hasn't made the connection clear."

"You're talking to God about it?"

Busted. "Yeah, some. Isn't that what we're supposed to do?"

"People who actually care what God's will is for their life do tend to ask for guidance in areas like marriage, yes."

"Wow, that was a careful answer. What makes you think I don't care? Just because I never did before doesn't mean a guy can't change."

"Have you? Changed, I mean?"

Should he be offended that his little brother couldn't see it, or thankful they were having a real conversation without jabbing at each other? They'd gotten that out of their system during their one-on-one. He met Alex's gaze. "Yeah, I'd like to think I have. I came home to make things right."

Alex's eyebrows flicked up just a hair. "Oh, yeah?"

"You know. Dixie and Dan."

"Right."

"I, uh, haven't gotten around to having a heart-to-heart with Mom and Dad yet." He'd been going to the other day, but Dad had been delayed because of a hurricane in Florida. Airline pilots didn't exactly work a nine-to-five.

"Interesting."

Was Alex hinting Basil should apologize to him? Probably. And it wasn't unwarranted. "Look, I know I haven't been the best big brother, and I certainly haven't been a good example. I'm sorry about that."

That hadn't been too hard.

Alex thumped his back. "You're forgiven. You didn't exactly lead me astray."

"No. Instead you decided to do the opposite of whatever I did."

"Pretty much." Alex smirked. "But I'm really thankful you moved back and are getting things in line. I wasn't sure what all went into that. Besides, I guess, buying back into Bridgeview Backyards."

Alex had been an original investor back when he'd bought his house and Peter lived with him. The business had started by taking over Alex's backyard growing produce for the CSA. Then Peter had married Sadie, who lived next door, and the expansion had begun.

And then Basil's DUI had blown everything.

He shoved the thought aside. He'd also apologized to Peter and Jasmine for leaving them in the lurch back then. It was over and done with. He couldn't change anything. All he could do now was pick up the pieces and make amends as best he could.

Alex snapped his fingers. "I know!"

"Know what?"

"Hailey North. That's who you should date. I've never figured out why you'd go out with a thousand girls—"

"Slight exaggeration," Basil protested.

"Only slight — and why you never dated her."

He shrugged. "Personal stuff." Hopefully that was nonchalant enough.

Alex raised his eyebrows. "What do you know about Hailey that I don't?"

Oh, lots of things. But this conversation was over. Had to be over. "You said you were in an all-fired hurry to get home. I should do the same. I need a shower."

"You sure do." Alex studied him a moment longer. "Think about Hailey. Pray about her. I don't know why I didn't see it before, but I bet you two would be perfect for each other."

"You've got rocks in your head." Basil managed a laugh. "Thanks for the game."

"I think you meant to say, 'thanks for the trouncing.' To which I'll respond, sure, anytime." Alex headed up the hill toward his house, his chuckle lingering in the air.

Basil spun the ball on the tip of his finger as he watched his brother leave. Was he such an open book that everyone could see how he and Hailey were meant for each other?

He didn't dare tell Alex, but thinking about Hailey and praying for her were at the top of his thoughts. All day, every day.

16

*F*ran caught on quickly, which was a huge relief as Kass was only managing a couple of hours here and there at work. If the staff had clued in that all the blame couldn't be laid on little Eleanor's teething problems, no one commented. It might help that most of them weren't mothers.

Hailey wanted to ask Kass if this much exhaustion and sickness was normal for early pregnancy, but she didn't really want to get too personal on this topic. She remembered the early sensations like they were yesterday: the tender breasts, the bloating, the nausea. Just thinking about it brought everything back.

But now it was Saturday afternoon, and they'd dismissed the last of their customers. She'd sent Kass home while she and Marley and Gabriella began the shutdown.

"Here, I'll help move the tables."

Hailey froze at Basil's voice from behind her. Of course, he'd come in the backdoor. Of course, he was ready to prepare for cutting holes in the exterior wall, even though Zeke would actually wield the saws.

He brushed past her, hip-checked his cousin Gabby out of the way, and lifted the other end of the table from Hailey. "Where's this going?"

"Uh, just ten feet back." She lifted, and they carried it together while the girls grabbed the next one.

It only took a few minutes to remove all the tables and chairs from the space then the items off the display shelves. Nothing on the café walls could be guaranteed safe from the vibrations. Zeke and his crew began installing the plastic barrier to keep the worst of the debris and dust from getting all over everything.

There was going to be a ton of dust, regardless. How could there not be, when the guys were cutting ginormous holes in brick walls?

"Anything else you need, Hailey?" asked Marley when the space had been cleared.

"No, it looks good. Thanks, both of you. It'll look a lot different in here when you come back on Tuesday."

"Can't wait!" Gabby bounced on her toes. "If you need a hand scrubbing Monday night, let me know. I could put in a couple of hours."

It would make up for her lost hours today. Hailey nodded. "Thanks. I'll let you know."

The two young women exited through the kitchen. Hailey should go, too. At the very least, she should head upstairs and change her clothes. But, somehow, she couldn't bring herself to leave. It wasn't just that the precious building she and Kass had inherited from their grandparents was going to have two holes carved in it. She also didn't want to think about how she felt watching Basil's muscles rippling under his gray T-shirt as he worked with Zeke.

Until he turned and caught her, a knowing smirk crossing his face.

She wanted to wipe the smugness from his face. Or kiss it off. No, not that. Okay, yes, totally. Would it really be so horrible to let this thing with him go somewhere? To find out what the possibilities were?

But he wanted his parents to know about their history. Then she'd have to tell Kass. And Jasmine. And... no. She'd done such a good job keeping everything hidden for twelve entire years. No one suspected a thing. She'd like to keep it that way.

"Is this too far to the left, Hailey?" Basil's eyebrows hiked up.

She glared at him. "It's fine."

"Oh, I thought I saw some hand signals there."

Very funny. She pivoted and marched to the counter before glancing over again.

He was already back to work, so she paused, watching his lithe, confident movements. Basil was no longer the carefree college dropout he'd been in Venice. He was no longer the guy who drifted aimlessly from one job to the next, who drank too much, who refused to take anything seriously.

Basil had grown up. Like, *really* grown up. A lot. He was fit and strong and focused... and he was even more gorgeous than he'd been at twenty-one. The man who signaled through the window then stood back, hands on his tool-belt-clad hips, was lean and strong. Her fingers itched to play with the black curly hair that peeked out beneath the hard hat he wore.

It wasn't just her fingers longing to get close. She closed her eyes, remembering how he'd held her tenderly while she blubbered all over him at the park. Why did she keep pushing him away? What was she so afraid of?

Of everyone finding out what she'd done. Not just that she and Basil had spent a carefree, careless summer. That was on both of them. So was the pregnancy. But what she'd done next... that was all on her. On her and on her parents, who were coming in just a few days now.

The whine of a power saw shattered the quiet, and Hailey jumped, refocusing on the work area beyond the plastic barrier. She really should go away. It wasn't like she could do anything to help right now, even if she wore protective gear like Basil and the crew.

He glanced over.

Caught her staring. Again.

Basil gave her a thumbs-up and turned back to where the saw tip emerged through the exterior wall.

Hailey darted through the bakery's kitchen and up the stairs to her apartment. It was going to be loud in there, too, but at least she wouldn't have to stare at Basil's muscles.

⌒⌇⌐

BASIL HADN'T CAUGHT another glimpse of Hailey since Saturday, and it wasn't for lack of proximity. He'd worked alongside Zeke all weekend, clearing debris, loading dumpsters, installing both the glass door to the exterior stairwell and the French doors to the patio, and fitting trim around them.

Hailey must have checked in to observe the progress

from time to time, but he hadn't caught her. Not since Saturday when she'd been ogling him.

He'd been working here for several weeks now, in and out, up and down the stairs, and he was no closer to a future with her than when he'd started. Possibly, he was further away, since they'd finally talked about things that night at Morley's, and then she'd made it clear she saw no future with him.

She was wrong. She had to be. How long could a woman hold that much pain close to herself and not let anyone in? Not move forward? If she could do it for a dozen years, could she do it for a lifetime? Maybe.

But he wanted more. He wanted *together*. They'd wasted enough time, hadn't they?

Was this at all how God felt about him? And how had God got Basil's attention? Just loving him. From a distance, when necessary, yet flooding Basil's heart and mind with warmth when he began giving God furtive glances again.

So that meant Basil needed to be patient. Needed to just keep being there for Hailey.

The thought of these feelings being love was no longer shocking. It was only truth. He loved her. He had, ever since that summer, albeit very imperfectly. He'd had to grow up to realize what he'd used and tossed aside. How valuable she was.

Her car was out back, so she was home. He'd take a chance.

Basil mounted the steps and knocked on her door, half expecting her to ignore him. She was good at that. He blinked as the door opened, revealing the woman who never left his thoughts. She wore shorts and a burnt-orange sleeveless top, her short hair tucked behind her ears.

"Oh, it's you."

"You don't need to sound so excited to see me," he teased.

She looked past him. "I hoped you were Kass, that's all."

He spread his hands wide. "It's your lucky day. You've got me instead."

Her eyebrows quirked, and he'd swear that was a grin trying to curve her mouth.

"I came to offer you a grand tour of your new space. Ready?"

"Um, sure. But Kass..."

Basil raised his eyebrows. "You know you want to see it now. Unless you've got a secret camera installed down there."

Okay, that *was* a smirk. "I wouldn't tell you if I did."

He chuckled. "I don't suppose you would. Does the feed play out on your TV or on your computer?"

"Wouldn't you like to know?"

Basil looked past her at the immaculate apartment. It was just as bright and cheery as the bistro downstairs. He'd bet her sofa was comfy. He could imagine curling up with Hailey on it, snuggled into that colorful quilt, watching a movie.

Hailey waved a hand across his line of vision, and he blinked.

Caught. "Come on. Let me show you." He extended his hand to her.

She slipped past him and pulled the door shut, leaving them together on the small windowed landing. She wrapped both arms around her middle instead of taking his hand. "Up or down?"

"Hmm." Basil pretended to think. "Up, first." He

followed her up the familiar stairs, failing to keep his mind on what he was supposed to be doing. It was hard to focus at the moment.

They emerged in the shadows beside the mechanical room, facing the semi-open kitchenette with its stainless counter, sink, and coffee station.

Hailey stepped out into the dining area interspersed with raised beds then stopped abruptly.

Basil caught her waist in his hands to avoid running her over. She stiffened. So did he, but he didn't let go, not with the heat from the back of her radiating over his chest and the smell of her shampoo filling his nostrils. "Hey."

She pushed at his hands, but not like she meant it. Right? He'd know. And then she wouldn't hesitate with her hands in place over his. She wouldn't lean back, ever so slightly.

He closed his eyes and breathed her in for the few seconds before she stepped away from him. "It looks nice up here." She sounded breathless.

Basil could relate. "*You* look nice."

"I'm talking about the rooftop patio."

"I'm not."

"Basil, I..." She stood a few feet away and turned halfway toward him. "Don't. Please."

"Hailey." He closed the gap. His palms craved the feel of her hips, so he rested them there. Her lips weren't far from his. Ever since that night in the park, he'd regretted not kissing her. He hadn't wanted to rush her. Had thought he'd get another chance within the next day or two. Instead, she'd retreated.

Now he lowered his mouth to hers, slowly enough she could get away if she really wanted to, but quickly enough that she didn't have a lot of time to decide. Neither did he. It was time to claim the woman he loved.

His lips lit on fire as they touched hers. His hands slid up her back and clutched her tight. The tiny bit of him that retained conscious thought realized her arms had come up around his neck, that her fingers tangled in the curls at his nape.

Basil groaned and deepened the kiss, tasting her, savoring her, feeling her need match his own. So much for her trying to convince him whatever they'd once shared was dead and gone. It was very much alive, and he didn't want to stop kissing her lest she pull away again. He didn't want to stop kissing her for any reason at all.

"Hailey?" a woman shrieked.

Okay, maybe for that reason. Basil didn't recognize the voice.

Hailey must have, because she reacted so quickly, he nearly landed on his duff. "Mom?"

Oh, boy. What a way to meet the parents. Or, more accurately, meet them again. There'd been that day the diplomats had taken a short break from their duties and surprised Hailey in Venice.

Basil and Hailey had just awakened. Thankfully, he'd been clothed and been ready to run down to the bakery at street level for pastries and caffè latte for a late breakfast. He'd opened the door to see her parents poised to knock. They'd stared at each other in shock.

Today, like then, there'd been no knock.

And it looked nearly as bad.

Hailey brushed past him as though he were insignificant and embraced the woman, then the man.

But her father kept his eyes focused on Basil. "Hailey Ann. It seems there's something you forgot to mention."

"Good afternoon, Mr. North." Basil's left hand found the small of Hailey's back as he straightened his shoulders and extended his right hand. "Basil Santoro."

"Again?" Mrs. North — Louise, right? — looked aghast between them. "I thought you said there was nothing further between you."

Hailey shifted away from Basil. "There wasn't. There isn't. It's not what it looked like."

Oh, it had very much been what it looked like. "On the contrary, Hailey's just in shock from your unexpectedly early arrival." He stressed the word early. "Being as you're here now, though, I'd love to spend some time together and get to know you, because I'd like to ask Hailey to marry me, and I'd appreciate your blessing on that."

"Basil!" Hailey all but hissed his name. "This is not—"

Eyebrows hiked, the man looked Basil up and down but said nothing as he slid both hands into his suit pants pockets, leaving Basil's hand in mid-air. Alrighty then.

"It's okay, love." Basil turned to Hailey. "I just wanted to lay my cards on the table, so your parents know where we stand."

"It's *not* where we stand." Hailey stretched her hands toward her mother then let them fall. "I can't believe... I'm sorry. I wasn't expecting you until next weekend."

"That's quite clear," her dad said, his voice dripping ice cubes down Basil's back.

There might be no blessing from this set of parents.

And Hailey might not forgive him for jumping the gun.

Way to go, Basil. Act first, speak second, think later. Repent at leisure.

17

*T*he events of the past five minutes swirled around Hailey's mind in slow motion. Basil. The amazing, electrifying kiss. And her parents, a full five days early. Basil's brash declaration — proposal? — in front of them.

He didn't mean it. He didn't want to marry her. Not Basil Santoro, playboy of Bridgeview. And she didn't want to marry him back, anyway. Not after the sardonically amused treatment over the past twelve years.

How dare he think he could slip back into her life after all this time and pick up where he'd left off? That kiss had shot fireworks through her entire body. And, yeah, she'd given as good as she'd gotten.

Mom and Dad.

Hailey closed her eyes, still swaying from the enormity of it all. And there was still Basil's hand on the small of her back. Just a little spot of warmth and assurance and solidarity, even though she'd denied his declaration.

Marry Basil? She couldn't. Wouldn't. But wasn't it just

her pride speaking by now? Because he'd proved, over and over this summer, that he'd changed.

"This rooftop never looked so good." Ever the diplomat, Mom pivoted slowly to study the space. "I like what you've done here."

Hailey opened her mouth to reply, but Basil beat her to the punch. "I'm glad you think so. It was a joint effort between Ranta Landscaping, Zeke's Construction, and Bridgeview Backyards, of which I'm part-owner. I had a lot of input into the design, all of it based on your daughter's vision."

"My brother mentioned what you were doing." Dad focused on Hailey, ignoring Basil's explanation. "Farrell said Kassidy invited them for the Grand Re-Opening on Tuesday, while *your* parents didn't even know there was a renovation going on."

Although Farrell and Lenore lived in Galena Landing, Idaho, they were a far greater part of Hailey's life than her own parents. Which wasn't really her fault. She hadn't mentioned the situation to Mom and Dad because she hadn't thought they'd care, one way or the other.

"Then it must be an awesome surprise," Basil announced cheerfully. "We're expecting this area to be a three-season addition, along with the new patio wedged in the space beside the business building next door. Not sure if you saw that on your way by. Zeke's Construction put in a timeless brick wall with a tall, wrought-iron gate along West Main. We can't wait to see what our regulars think of it all tomorrow." He slid his arm around Hailey's waist. "Right, honey?"

The instant stretched. She should step away and unequivocally deny the connection. Maybe she should even slap his smug face to make sure he and Dad both got the message.

But... she couldn't do that to Basil. She hadn't been able to shake him from her thoughts since his return to Bridgeview — and she'd done a lousy job of it all twelve years before that. This new thing between them, this new strand linking them, was too fragile, too tenuous, for a quick reaction.

And it was too late, anyway. Basil's hand settled on her hip, and he'd shifted a teensy bit closer, as though it were a comfortable, natural position. Was it? Could it be?

Part of her yearned to move forward from that kiss, to agree with Basil's assumption of marriage, and let go of all the tightly held memories and pain. God forgave them, even though they'd known better at the time. Maybe Basil hadn't acted out of rebellion as she had. Scratch that. He had, too. So, how could God forgive? The Bible didn't differentiate between unknowing or rebellious sin, as far as she could tell. The forgiveness was for all.

She lacked the courage to forgive herself.

Mom feigned a yawn with a pat to her lips. "I'm sorry, darling, it's been a long day. I hope your guest room is ready. I could use a little rest before dinner."

It was nearly eight o'clock. Hailey'd eaten leftovers from the bistro walk-in two hours ago. She forced a smile. "Sure. Come on down to the apartment." She took a step toward the staircase, but somehow Basil stayed right with her.

"Want me to order Italian?" he asked quietly. "I can get Tony to toss something together."

Her parents preceded them into the stairwell, and Hailey stopped to look at Basil. "Why are you doing this?"

"Doing what?"

"Don't even pretend. You know we're not a couple—"

He brushed his lips over hers for one tantalizing second. "That's not what your kiss told me."

"It was a mistake." But her voice lacked conviction.

"Hailey." Basil's hand brushed the side of her cheek, electrifying all those nerve endings again. "The time of denial is past. Let me do this for you. Let me show you how much I care."

It was either that or face her parents alone for the remainder of the evening, to say nothing of the entire week of their planned visit. Though, since they'd arrived early, were they staying two weeks? Please, no.

"We need to talk."

His eyes gleamed as his mouth turned up in a grin. "Now you're speaking my language." He dropped a quick kiss to her mouth and nudged her toward the stairs. "After you."

BASIL PULLED multiple containers of aromatic Italian dishes out of the bags on Hailey's counter. He hadn't been this far into her apartment before, something her parents would no doubt have difficulty believing.

"Bless Tony," murmured Hailey, breathing in the fragrant steam with her eyes closed.

Basil grinned. "Yup. Handy to have a cousin who owns a restaurant only a couple of blocks away."

Mr. North had loosened his tie while Basil was gone, but that was the only indication the couple was settling in for the night. They both watched from the sofa as Hailey set plates and silverware on the counter.

"Come and help yourselves," Basil invited. "I'd be happy to say grace, unless you'd like to, Edgar?"

He heard Hailey's sharp inhale beside him, but kept his gaze fixed on her dad.

The man narrowed his gaze at him as he rose from the sofa. "Go ahead."

Basil kept it short and sweet, but he was going to do a lot more praying silently. No wonder Hailey'd been so messed up. These people projected disapproval and even disdain to a degree Basil had rarely experienced. And that was to their own daughter, not some random, snarky stranger.

Louise North looked over the offerings. "This doesn't look authentic. What is this?"

"My cousin Tony offers numerous keto options at his Italian restaurant. I wasn't sure if you'd prefer zucchini noodles or regular pasta, so I picked up some of each. Even my very Italian nonna approves."

That was a bit of a stretch. Nonna had certainly argued with Tony's menu at first, but finally conceded that people in weight-loss mode, like Peter's wife, Sadie, might deserve to eat out occasionally without feeling sabotaged. Sadie had lost well over a hundred pounds a couple of years ago with the Trim Healthy Mama way of eating, and she'd won Nonna over... at least, to a degree.

Hailey's mom reached for the fettuccine as though the zucchini would bite her. At least she wasn't rejecting the entire meal.

Basil scooped a large portion of zucchini to a plate and offered it to Hailey with his eyebrows raised.

"I think I'll have rotini tonight," she said, picking up another plate.

"More veggies for me!" Basil reached for the pasta server and set pasta on her plate. "How about some creamy thyme sauce on that?"

Her eyes implored him to stop, but he couldn't. Her parents needed to see him firmly in Hailey's corner, whether she realized it or not.

"Thyme is a staple of Italian cooking, right up there with basil." No one laughed. Okay, the attempt at a joke had been rather awkward. "Did you know thyme represents strength and fortitude? Courage, really."

"Basil..." Hailey breathed in a warning tone.

"Here you go. A heaping helping of courage." He ladled the creamy sauce over Hailey's pasta.

"Stop."

Her dad turned back from the other end of the counter next to the Caprese. "Do you have any red wine?"

"No, sir," Basil interjected before Hailey could speak. Maybe she had some in the apartment. He didn't know. "I used to drink rather too much, and it's best if I steer clear of alcohol now."

Edgar's eyebrows rose slowly as he looked down his nose at Basil. "That is not my problem."

"Dad, please." Hailey took a shuddering breath. "No, I don't have any wine at the moment. Remember, I didn't know you were coming this early. We can pick some up tomorrow. I'll pour ice water for everyone."

"Go ahead and have a seat, love." Basil nudged her toward the table. "I'll get the water."

Hailey's glare showed she planned to murder him later.

He winked, but she only took a deep breath and shook her head as she turned aside. Why couldn't her parents have stayed away until their planned arrival? He hadn't even had time to show Hailey the rest of the finishing touches of the renovation. Thankfully, he hadn't dawdled on the opportunity to kiss her.

She'd been into it, hadn't she? She had. Then why was she pretending they meant nothing to each other in front of her parents? The parents who'd witnessed the passionate kiss that would keep Basil awake all night. They wouldn't be fooled.

But they knew about the pregnancy. The abortion. They wouldn't be predisposed to welcome Basil into the family circle — not that they really had one, from all Hailey had said in Venice and from the evidence of their few visits here in the intervening years.

He filled four glasses with ice and water, carried them to the table, and set them at each place. He'd have been a more debonair server with a platter and a white towel, but it was going to take more than his experience at the Fireweed to impress the Norths.

Louise nibbled at the Calabrese salad and her fettuccine a la puttanesca.

Looked like it was going to be up to Basil to carry the conversation. "So, where have you been stationed most recently?"

Edgar glanced at him. "That's classified."

Okay. "Have you been back in the States long?"

"Just a couple of days."

The man was not going to make this easy. "Well, you've sure picked a nice time of year to visit Spokane. It's a little cooler in September than it was earlier, and nights cool off nicely. It—"

"I grew up here," Edgar interrupted. "I know about seasons in eastern Washington."

"Great!" Basil managed to infuse a little enthusiasm in his response, but it was painful. He focused on the spiralized zucchini and thyme sauce. Wouldn't it be nice if the medieval tales of thyme building courage were true... and instant? Because he could sure use a shot of assurance that went deeper than this show of bravado he was engaged in. If only he and Hailey'd had a chance to talk about that kiss. Talk about their feelings.

Basil nearly scoffed aloud but managed to cough instead. He was a goner if he wanted to talk about emotional stuff.

"So." Edgar folded his napkin and set it aside, turning to Basil. "Why is this the first I've heard of your undying devotion to my daughter? You are the same scoundrel from the summer Hailey spent in Italy, are you not?"

"Yes, sir. The very same." Basil didn't dare glance at Hailey. "Please understand I was just a kid myself back then and not on a very good path. I drifted a lot since then, as well, so I wouldn't blame you for thinking I might not be good enough for your daughter."

The man's eyebrows peaked.

"But things have changed." Did he have to tell the whole tale? If things with Hailey progressed — and Basil meant them to, for sure — everything would come out sooner or later. Better now. "A few years ago, I was convicted of driving under the influence. I spent ninety days in jail, paid a fine, and lost my driver's license for two years. I was very bitter, as you might imagine."

Louise set her fork down, watching Basil as closely as her husband did. Hailey had eaten maybe three bites. Now her eyes were closed. Hopefully, she was praying. Courage wasn't all he needed. He could sure use some divine intervention, as well.

"But that all gave me some time to think about the trajectory my life was on. I realized I didn't like the guy I'd become. I talked to God about it, and He told me to come home. That seemed to mean back to Bridgeview... and back to my childhood faith."

Hailey peered at him through lowered lashes, but he kept his focus on her dad.

"That's what brought me home a couple of months ago now, and brought me back into Hailey's life. I knew I needed to apologize to her for the events of that summer." Basil hesitated. "I'd like to think I would have been there for her had I known the chaos that reigned after I left, but I'm honestly not sure."

"You were an immature, spoiled child."

"Yes, sir. I was. And I'm sorry."

"You've done enough damage." Louise rose slowly, her gaze skewering Basil. "I think you should leave."

He glanced at Hailey's ashen face, but she didn't meet his eyes. "I'll be happy to go as soon as I've cleaned up from dinner, but I want you to know — I'll be back. Because Hailey means everything to me."

"Thanks, Basil, but I've got it." Hailey stood, not looking at him, and reached for her mother's plate. "I think we've said everything we need to say today."

"If you wish." He had more food on his plate, but his appetite seemed to have vanished. "I'll see you tomorrow."

Hailey darted a glance at him as though questioning the wisdom of that.

He pressed a quick kiss to her cheek. "I wouldn't miss the Grand Re-Opening for anything."

18

*H*ailey slipped down to the bakery kitchen at her usual time and set up the coffee pot they kept in the staff room. Had she slept at all? It seemed she'd noted every hour from when she'd excused herself shortly after Basil left until her alarm rang. Whatever time zone her parents were on, they'd retired early — and silently — and not been stirring when she rose.

Now she had an hour before Reina arrived. Time to set the breads, buns, and cinnamon rolls to rising. They'd go through more than usual with the Grand Re-Opening today. At least, she hoped so, or it would all have been a waste.

She purged Basil, along with her parents, from her thoughts and focused on the daily tasks she knew so well.

Bless Basil's cousin Brittany. She hadn't worked for Hailey and Kass as much as her sister Gabriella or cousin Ava had, but the girl had mad baking skills and loved to be turned loose in the kitchen at times. She'd come in yesterday and baked dozens of cookies they would use as doorbusters today. Today, she'd man the table offering a free coffee and cookie to anyone who wanted one. The fancy drinks and the remainder of the inventory, including the dozens of cupcakes Brittany had baked and decorated, would be for sale.

Hailey wished, not for the first time, that they'd been able to entice Brittany to make baking a career with her and Kass, but no. The young woman worked as a graphic artist for an established Spokane ad agency and indulged in baking on the side.

At least she'd been willing to help out with today's extravaganza. Nearly everyone who'd ever worked at Bridgeview Bakery and Bistro would be back for the day. Kass's husband, Wesley, would be bussing tables, and even her stepmom, Lenore, would help cover the lunch hours, since she'd worked here several months a couple of years ago.

Hailey and Kass had tried to plan for a crazy successful day. It was the unexpected stuff she was worried about. She wasn't dumb enough to think that having a plan was enough... even though running without expanded staff and additional baking would have been ridiculous.

Hailey weighed out dough and formed loaves of their signature sourdough whole-grain breads and tried to squelch the anxiety that wanted to rise. The upbeat worship music coming through the speakers filtered into her mind, and she began to sing along out loud. No one was around to hear whether she was on tune or not. Probably not, but it didn't matter. The lyrics helped center her thoughts.

"Hailey?"

She whirled toward the alley door to see Basil standing just inside. "Oh, my word. You gave me quite a start."

"Sorry. I came to see if I could give you a hand."

She blinked the clock into focus. Not quite five o'clock. Reina would be in soon. "I—"

He scrubbed up at the sink. "Just put me to work. Is everything ready out front?"

"Shay will be in at six to put the chairs back down and fill the display cases." Closing shift always upended the chairs when they mopped the floors. "And Astrid is starting at seven today."

Basil's eyebrows rose. "I don't know why you keep her around. She's... abrasive."

"Yeah, well, I happen to agree with you, but the regulars seem to like her, all the same. At first, I think she was just around to keep an eye on Kass and make sure she was fit to be stepmom for Astrid's grandson, but she does a decent job of serving our clients, so..." Hailey shrugged. "It's not like we have too many employees."

"I guess." Basil dried his hands. "Okay, what do you want me to do?"

"I have a list. Don't distract me."

He chuckled. "I'll try not to, even though distraction is part of my beguiling charm."

"You really messed with my parents' heads last night."

"Oh? What did they say?" He studied her whiteboard with its to-do list. "Can I start the muffins?"

"Reina will do those." Seriously, why was he here? She needed to focus. Today was not the day to forget or double an ingredient.

"Tell me what your parents said."

"They don't trust your motives."

"Do you?"

Oh, how she wanted to give him a flippant reply, but she bit her lip instead.

"Hailey?"

She measured off a hunk of dough and began rolling it out. "I'm not sure."

"My reasons are actually fairly straightforward, like I mentioned to your dad. I want to earn your trust and your love, and I want to marry you."

"Basil..." Good thing she could spread butter on the dough without overthinking it. She didn't dare look at him, though she sensed he'd moved to her side of the worktable.

"But, the main thing for today is that I know it's a big day for you, and I want to support you in that. It's a chance to work on that first step, earning your trust."

Hailey reached for the brown sugar and cinnamon mix. "Great, but honestly? I need to focus."

"I'll take that *great* for now."

Impossible man.

He looked through the doorway into the quiet café. "Do you have flowers coming for the tables?"

Flowers! Ack, that was something she or Kass should have thought of. "No."

"If I really can't help you in the kitchen...?"

She huffed. "You can't."

"Then I'll do flowers. Got any of those mini vases?"

"No. We don't do flowers often, but we do have a bunch of little canning jars. One-cuppers, I think. They're probably on the top shelf of the storeroom."

Basil saluted before striding across the space and into the supply room. A moment later he came back out with a couple of boxes. "These?"

She nodded as she began to roll the dough over the toppings.

"Don't worry about a thing. I've got this. Be right back."

Not worry about anything? Well, it wasn't the flowers that caused concern, though she had no idea where he'd source them before the bistro opened at seven. But she totally trusted him to come up with something amazing.

That left worrying about *him*. About whether it was wise to have a relationship with him. Whether it would blow her life wide open.

No, she knew it would. Also, it didn't matter if it was *wise* or not — they had a relationship, anyway. Venice had seen to that. But the memories had escaped their bounds and been released in present time.

Oh, that kiss. Those promises. The touch on her lower back. The amazing food he'd brought over from Antonio's with half an hour's notice.

Maybe she needed to infuse thyme into everything in her life. She could sure use the courage.

WHISTLING TO HIMSELF, Basil arranged the flowers he'd found in the community garden into the small jars, adding a sprig of herbs to each. He had the rooftop patio to himself for a few minutes more and, even now, he could hear voices from the sidewalk down below. Folks were waiting to enter when one of the workers — probably not Hailey — unlocked the doors and ushered them in.

He was no florist, that was for sure. Casual. He was going for casual. And goodness, he'd cut a lot of flowers. He'd counted the tables and the jars and, even if he stuffed every jar to the point of ridiculous, there were too many blossoms.

Basil's eye caught on one of the large glass pitchers on

the shelf above his head. One of those... he pulled it down and arranged the last of the mums and asters into a full bouquet. He smirked as he buried a few tendrils of thyme amid the blossoms. He'd give that to Hailey later. Would she catch the double meaning?

"Basil?" Shay crossed the rooftop from the outside stairs. "Wow, those look great! I'm about ready to unlock the doors and was just checking that everything was ready up here. Ava's going to cover this area. She's just getting her apron on."

"All is well. I was just about to set the flowers out."

"I'll grab this tray. Enough for the main dining area?"

Basil nodded. "I'll get these up here and the patio down there."

"Perfect." Shay lifted the tray and took a few steps toward the stairs. "I'm not sure why you're here, but I'm glad you are. Hailey needs some sunshine in her day. I've never seen her so stressed out."

Probably her parents' arrival more than anything else, but he wouldn't mention that to Shay. Instead, he bobbed his eyebrows. "Sunshine? That's my job. If you need a court jester, just give me a call."

She chuckled and headed down.

Basil took the other tray and began setting out the jars of flowers. Yeah, that was the finishing touch the rooftop needed. Inside might not need it as much, since the decor was more colorful to start with. Once he'd set all the tables, he headed to the street-level patio to do the same, listening to the voices and laughter swell on the other side of the brick fence.

And then Shay unlocked the door, and the crowd

poured in. Some immediately came onto the patio while others mounted the stairs.

"Welcome!" Ava announced. Great. The rooftop was in good hands.

Basil excused himself past the lineup waiting for their complimentary coffee and cookie and tucked the tray back where he'd found it. Now what could he do? Looked like Brittany could use a hand with the freebies. He stepped up beside her and took the tongs from her hand. "Let me help."

He set a cookie on a napkin and handed it to the next person in line as Britt poured coffee from the tall urn. She flashed him a smile. "Thanks, cuz."

"No prob." He passed over the next cookie. "Good morning, Mr. Ito."

His nonna's old friend smiled and nodded his thanks. The Robertsons were next, then a few of the teachers from Bridgeview Elementary, then Dad and his brothers.

Basil couldn't have said how many cookies he passed out, but he was on his fourth container when his smile froze at the sight of Hailey's parents across the serving table. "Good morning, Edgar, Louise. I hope you slept well."

Hailey's dad stared at him for a second. "Well enough."

That made one of them. Basil had barely snatched a wink between worrying about Hailey, panicking that he'd been too cocky and blown his chances, and praying about it all a hundred times. Now he glanced around the bustling bistro and to the patio beyond. A couple was in the process of vacating the space. "I believe there are open tables outside."

Hailey's mother gave him a quizzical look before

murmuring her thanks for the coffee and following her husband between the tables.

Basil caught the questioning look his own father passed to the strangers. Between Dad and the uncles, they probably knew every single other person who'd come in the door, so an outsider would catch his attention.

Finally, the line slowed, and more tables became vacant as some of the folks headed off to start their days.

"Are you on payroll today?" Brittany asked.

"Me?" Basil laughed. "Nope. Just helping out. You? I don't remember you working here."

"I help out once in a while, as needed. I've helped cater a few weddings and other events to pick up some loose change. That sort of thing."

There'd been several family weddings in the past few months. Hailey and Kass had catered Dominic and Katri's, but Alex and Marley's had been served by an outside company, as had Tony and Kenna's. Charlie and Aunt Winnie had married on a Florida beach and avoided the whole Santoro extravaganza.

Destination weddings weren't a bad idea. Maybe he could talk Hailey into Venice. Provided she'd say yes when he actually proposed.

Last night? That had been a trial run to get Hailey and her parents warmed up to the idea. Because Basil wasn't going anywhere. He was going to be right here in Bridgeview involved in Hailey's life until he'd convinced her he was a changed man and the best possible partner to stand by her side into their old age.

With that in mind, how was Hailey holding up? Basil hefted one of the several empty coffee urns. "I'll take these back to the kitchen and get them refilled for the lunch rush."

"Sure." Brittany gave him a side-eye. "I'm not sure what you've done with my cousin Basil, but you're a pretty nice guy, all things considered."

If his hands weren't full, he'd clap one to his chest melodramatically. As it was, he jiggled his eyebrows. "I've always been a nice guy."

She huffed a laugh. "You hid it well."

And that right there was what his extended family really thought of him. This core change was long overdue, but it was here now.

He carried the container into the kitchen, and Hailey glanced over. "Hey. What're you doing?"

"We've got a few empty urns out front, so I thought I'd clean them and get them prepped for the next rush. How are things back here?"

Hailey studied him for a few seconds. "We're keeping on top."

"Barely," muttered Reina.

"But we are. It's slowed down a little, right?"

Basil nodded.

"Whatever you're doing out there, thank you."

He flashed her a grin. "You're welcome. And I fixed a bouquet for you, too. Want it in here for now?"

Hailey blinked. "Uh... no. Too hot. But thanks."

"I'll put it in your office, then." Whatever she wanted, he'd give her. He'd been crazy to stick to his arrogant pride for so long instead of humbling himself and begging forgiveness and another chance years ago. But now that he was here? He wasn't giving up.

19

*I*f only Hailey could collapse with her feet up, but that was not to be. She'd stayed long after the lunch rush, since the orders kept rolling in from the front until they were all but out of food. And then she'd stayed to place orders so they could re-open in the morning with at least a semblance of a menu in place.

She sat at her desk in the bakery office and rubbed her temples. The thought of dragging herself up to her apartment sounded like it required too much energy. And her parents were likely sitting up there waiting to be served dinner. Maybe she could stretch out right here on the floor and pretend she didn't remember their presence.

The fragrance of the fall bouquet on her desk added to the lure of staying put.

"You okay?" Julissa stood in the office doorway.

"Define okay."

"Well, you must have made a ton of money today. So that's good, right?"

Was that the whole point of life? Today, Hailey didn't

much care. Well, scratch that. She'd served a few times at Blessings Under the Bridge, often enough to see how the homeless lived. But owning her own business and constantly pushing for the next level? She was over it.

Kass had been right when she suggested waiting until Saturday for the Grand Re-Opening party. Then they'd have had two days to recuperate. Hailey hadn't wanted to wait to show off the new spaces to the entire city. She should learn to listen to her cousin.

Julissa untied her apron. "Want me to get you something before I leave? A coffee? A sandwich? Anything?"

Hailey was pretty sure they were out of bread and buns but, if Julissa had closed the kitchen as always, sourdough was bubbling away for tomorrow's baking. It never ended.

She shook her head. "Thanks, but I don't think I could face a plate of anything."

Julissa frowned. "But you need to eat."

Did she? Her parents would think so. Maybe if she stayed here long enough, they'd go out for dinner and leave her in peace. If only.

She sighed. "I'm fine. See you tomorrow."

"See you then."

Hailey's cell rang as the backdoor clicked. She stared at Kass's face on the screen for a minute before tapping it. Kass had only lasted a couple of hours before going home and letting her staff take over. Hopefully she was okay. "Hi."

"Hailey, Wesley's heading over to pick you up. Your mom and dad are here visiting with my dad and Lenore. Lenore is making dinner, and you're coming. You don't need to stay long, but I know you, and I know you're exhausted and will likely avoid food if I don't make you eat. So just walk out the alley door and lock up and get in Wesley's truck. I won't take no for an answer."

The refusal died on Hailey's lips. Letting her cousin take care of her, even for a little while, was the best outcome she could hope for. Except Basil. Her eyes focused on the casual bouquet tucked in a glass pitcher. Basil had already done more for her today than nearly anyone else, and he'd done it without pay. He was trying to prove he'd changed. That he loved her.

It was working. She leaned closer to sniff the sweet fragrance, but there was something... different... about the aroma. What on earth?

"Hailey? Are you walking to the door yet?"

She heaved a deep sigh and pushed to her feet. "Okay. I am now."

"Good girl. I'll see you in five."

Except what was in the flowers? It smelled like an herb. Thyme. She laughed out loud. She could get a spurt of energy — or at least a flicker — from that unspoken message of courage. Crazy guy.

It seemed ridiculous for someone to drive three blocks to pick her up. She was perfectly capable of walking that far. Except that the two dozen steps to the back of the building were almost more than she could manage. She exited and locked the door while Wesley hopped out of his truck and opened the passenger door.

"Your chariot awaits."

She managed a sort of smile. "Thanks." Then she sagged back against the upholstery as though her bones were goo. "I should have gone upstairs to change. My hair's a mess and I smell like... I don't know what I smell like, but it can't be pretty." It wasn't flowers, and it wasn't thyme.

Wesley chuckled as he backed out of the parking spot. "You're fine. This isn't a public appearance, anyway. You're with family. No one's judging."

"My parents are."

He glanced across the cab and shrugged. "They'll have to go through me if that's how it's going to be."

"Aw. You're the best. Kass is lucky to have you in her corner."

"I'm thankful to God we found each other."

Hailey stared blankly out the window as they passed the riverside park then rounded the curve by Myles and Adriana's house. Wesley pulled into the driveway next door, and she pushed on the door handle. One hour. She could eat whatever was offered, smile and nod for a few minutes, then go home and crawl into bed. Her parents were going to have to look after themselves. They were good at it.

꩜

Wow, that had been a long day. Basil had made himself useful wherever he could. When things slowed enough that Brittany could easily manage the complimentary coffee bar on her own, he'd gone up top and pulled orders off the dumbwaiter so Ava had time to actually smile and say hello to the folks crowding the rooftop.

Then he'd repotted a planter of flowers on the street-level patio where someone's toddler had gone rogue and yanked out a dozen barely rooted seedlings. After that, he'd sold two of his sister-in-law's whimsical chicken paintings. Marley had mouthed *thank you* to him as he lifted them off the wall and taken them over to the cash register with the effusive older lady walking behind him, already digging into her purse.

Basil hiked up the hill quite a lot slower than usual, but it had been a good day. He'd looked around for Hailey before he left, but she must have gone upstairs. He'd text Hailey later, but she'd seemed beyond exhausted last he'd seen of her something like twelve hours into her shift.

His cousin Tony exited Nonna's house just as Basil came abreast of it. "Hey, cuz! How was the day down at the bistro?"

"Busy. Didn't I see you there?"

"I popped in for a couple of minutes, but it was crazy. I thought I'd take a tour and congratulate Kass and Hailey another time."

"Just as well. Even the slow times were crazy busy."

Tony laughed. "Good for them. I didn't know you were on payroll, though."

"Uh. I wasn't. I just helped out." *No need to ask why, buddy.*

"All day?" Tony's eyebrows shot up.

"Sure, why not? It's what friends do." At least, kissing friends. Would he get another chance for that anytime soon? Basil wasn't used to being nudged aside.

"Friends, hmm?" A sound behind him caused Tony to turn before looking back at Basil. "Oh, right. Nonna asked me to invite you in."

"I'm tired, or I'd comply."

"That's why she's inviting you. You wouldn't turn down fresh, warm struffoli, would you? When she made some just for you on a hot September day because she knows it's one of your favorites?"

Oh, that's how Nonna was playing it? And if Basil

insisted on going to his quiet apartment a couple of blocks away, she was going to take it personally? He lowered his voice. "How do you put up with her meddling ways?"

Tony grinned. "She loves us all, you know. Come on in for a few and take a load off your feet. It won't kill you."

Basil sighed and followed his cousin up the steps. Kenna had been Nonna's caregiver after a bad fall last summer, back when Tony was living in the basement and getting Antonio's off the ground. Now Tony and Kenna were married and still living with Nonna. Basil's mom tried to spin it as Nonna living with the young married couple, but Basil knew better. It was still Nonna's house, and she'd be running the household until she died.

"Basil, come in, come in." Nonna beckoned him from a tall stool by the kitchen island.

Kenna chopped vegetables across the island, her tongue caught between her teeth in concentration. Tony gave Kenna a quick hug then began pouring water in a large kettle.

"You will stay for dinner, si?"

Basil shifted from one foot to the other. "Uh, I wasn't planning on it. I have some leftovers at the apartment." Although, those were about four days old, and his enthusiasm for them was nonexistent.

"But you must eat, and Antonio and Makenna are cooking enough to share."

Tony grinned from over by the stove.

Just come in and say hi, right? Never that easy with Nonna.

"Ow!" Her eyes growing wide, Kenna dropped the knife and sucked on her finger.

Tony crossed the space and had a look at his wife's cut. "Let's get a sterile strip on that, love."

Nonna shook her head as the couple disappeared down the hallway. "That girl cannot cook to save her life."

Basil picked up the knife and finished chopping the celery she'd begun. Better that than sitting next to Nonna with nothing to do. And now that he was helping with the meal, he might as well stick around and enjoy it. As long as Tony was in charge, not his wife.

"So, was the bistro busy all day?" Nonna wanted to know.

"It was."

"And you work for them now? I thought you worked with Peter and Jasmine."

"I took the day off so I could help Hailey and Kass. I wanted to make sure the spaces were as functional in action as they'd looked in theory."

"Did they *need* help?"

Basil didn't shoot the look at his grandmother that he was tempted to. She'd probably read more into that glance than he'd be able to read on her face. "They could use about three or four more employees, honestly. But Fran is fitting in well. She did great today, as did the rest of your grand-daughters. Oh, and we sold a couple of Marley's paintings, too."

"That's good."

Basil swept the celery aside and started slicing the eggplant sitting beside the cutting board. That's why it was there, right? It would be quick to dice if that's what Tony wanted.

"So, you have returned to Bridgeview."

That hardly needed acknowledgment, so he just nodded. He'd been back for over a month.

"Why?"

And... why was he so afraid of his nonna? It wasn't like she was going to spank him or pinch his ear, though she'd probably thought about it. Basil set the knife down and studied her face across the island. "Because I missed my family and my community. And because I wanted a fresh start."

"Oh?"

"I don't need to tell you I was a mess, Nonna. I embarrassed the Santoro name, and I'm sorry."

She swept her hand aside. "It is just a name."

That hadn't been the party line while he'd been growing up, that's for sure.

Nonna met his gaze. "It is more important what God thinks than what your old nonna thinks."

"You're not old."

"I am eighty-one, so I am not young, either. I will die, and someday it will be your turn. What will God say when you meet Him? Will He say, 'well done, good and faithful servant,' or will He say, 'depart from me; I never knew you'?"

Wow, Nonna was cutting to the chase. "If it were today, I believe He'd have a third option."

"Oh?"

"I think He'd say, 'welcome back, Basil. You messed up, but you asked forgiveness, and My Son's death covers that for you.'"

Nonna reached across the island and covered his hand with her work-worn one. "If you have asked forgiveness, then He has given it and the first answer holds true. He does not hold a grudge as we are so good at. He forgives."

"Even when we don't deserve it?" Basil knew the answer, but it was so hard to grasp and not let go.

"None of us ever deserves it. God gives anyway. He gives freely to all who ask."

How he wished Hailey could see that. But it wasn't only for her. It was for him, too. He smiled at his grandmother. "Thanks for the reminder. For the confirmation."

"Now, I did not invite you inside so you could work some more. Come, sit down. Tony will be back in a minute, and he'll make dinner."

He came around the island and nudged Nonna's shoulder with his elbow. "He bribed me by saying you made struffoli."

"I am glad it worked. I wanted to see you, but you never stop by."

What did *God* bribe him with? Because God had felt the same way about Basil for many years. He wanted to spend time with Basil, but Basil avoided it.

Not anymore. On either count.

"Thanks, Nonna. I guess I can wait until after dinner."

She shifted on her stool to look down the hallway, where Tony and Kenna's low voices conversed. Then she leaned closer to Basil. "Have one now, quickly, and we'll save the rest for dessert."

Didn't that go a long way to make a guy feel like his nonna's favorite?

20

*H*ailey glanced up from her Bible app as her dad, still clad in his sleep pants, came in the kitchen on Sunday morning. "Coming to church? It starts at ten-thirty."

Dad yawned and patted his mouth. "Your mother didn't mention wanting to go."

"It would mean a lot to me." Hailey glanced at the bouquet beside her coffee cup. Maybe she could inhale a little of the courage Basil's thoughtful gesture had tucked inside. "I believe Uncle Farrell and Aunt Lenore will be going."

"She's not really your aunt, you know."

Hailey bit her tongue from the retort that wanted to come out. She settled for a mild, "She's married to your brother, and that makes her my aunt." What did it matter that she hadn't given birth to Kass? She'd been her stepmom since Kass had been five.

Dad rolled his eyes and reached for the coffee pot.

Hailey leaned in to sniff the flowers and herbs in the

arrangement. She'd be lying if she denied the little uplift every time she thought about the unwritten message Basil had tucked in the mix. Knowing he was on her side gave her the strength to smile and nod at her parents while trying not to let the conversation get too personal. It wasn't like they really cared about her. She'd always been little more than an inconvenience in their lives.

She hadn't seen much of Basil the past few days. She'd told him she was tired, that she was busy, that she needed to spend time with her parents. All that was true. Mostly, she hadn't had the chance to process the kiss last Monday evening or Basil's declaration to her parents.

But, he'd be at church. It was cowardly to hope her parents didn't come. They needed Jesus more than anyone else she knew. Her grandparents had raised their sons in the faith, but neither had followed through as adults. Uncle Farrell had recommitted his life to the Lord a couple of years back, though.

"I think we'll pass this time." Dad stirred a little cream into his brew, not meeting Hailey's gaze. "We thought we'd spend the entire day together. You work so much."

They were the ones who'd arrived on a Monday evening, knowing full well the bistro was open Tuesday through Saturday. "That comes from owning a business. Can't be helped."

"Maybe we'll go down to Riverside Park when you get home. We haven't taken the gondolas across the river in years. What do you think?"

She'd never go anywhere near that part of the park without a shudder at the memory of Holden's insistent lips. "Why don't you and Mom do that one day while I'm working? It's not much of a treat for me." Hailey hesitated. "You're staying a few more days, right?"

Dad focused on the view out the window. "We'll see. We're expected in L.A. Wednesday."

Hailey stared at him. "But your schedule... you came early. I thought that meant you'd stay longer."

"Things have come up. I wish you'd spend the day with us today."

"I'll be back right after church." If ever Hailey needed a lifeline, it was today. Thyme was great. She could smile and gather a little courage from Basil's belief in her, but what she really needed was some immersive time with the Lord. She couldn't let her parents take that away from her.

They'd already removed so much. Their own love. Her baby.

Yes, she'd had a choice, but she'd been young and wanting her parents' approval more than anything else. She'd never dreamed she'd be haunted by what she'd done for years. That it would affect every area of her life.

Yet, it was twelve years later, but she was barely beginning to heal. Because Basil had forgiven her, though he'd struggled with it. Of course, he'd wrestled. What upstanding person wouldn't? Which only proved her parents weren't.

She glanced at the clock. "I should start getting ready. You've got twenty minutes to change your mind."

Dad harrumphed and carried his coffee to the other room.

Alrighty, then.

BASIL EDGED past Alex and Marley to squeeze next to Hailey in the middle of the pew. Who cared what others thought of seeing them together? Maybe she cared, but too bad. He was in full pursuit, and she wouldn't dare get up and walk away from him as music filled the sanctuary.

Logan leaned into the microphone as his hands traveled the keyboard of the grand piano. "Welcome, friends and neighbors. We're here to worship God this morning, so won't you join me in singing 'Good, Good Father'?"

Basil loved this one. He joined right in, but Hailey didn't. She might not have the greatest voice, but didn't she usually sing? He was sure she did. But then he thought about the lyrics as they rolled across the screen and considered Edgar North.

Hailey's father was a far cry from Basil's. Raimondo Santoro had been an exemplary dad, hands-on, always there. Okay, maybe not that last bit. Dad's career as an airline pilot meant he'd missed more of his kids' basketball games and other events than he wished as he worked his way up the ladder. Basil had resented that in his early teens. He hadn't understood the balance of work and home, even though Dad had apologized profusely.

But Hailey's dad hadn't even popped in several times a week. She'd been lucky to see him every couple of years when he'd taken a week of leave. What did a good, good father even look like to Hailey?

He shot her a sidelong glance to find her looking down at her tightly entwined fingers. The impulse to cover her hands with his nearly overcame him, but caution overruled. Even worse was the desire to slide his arm around her shoulder and pull her tight. Instead, he increased the pressure of his arm against hers. They were already wedged into the pew like sardines, so no one should notice that little extra contact.

No one except Hailey. She peeked at him, her lip trembling slightly.

"Hey," he whispered. "You okay?"

Her shoulder moved against his in the slightest shrug. She was *not* okay.

There wasn't much he could do about it at the moment. Well, he could pray for her. This whole thing seemed new, though he'd been walking in practice of his childhood faith for a couple of months now.

The words of the worship song washed over him as he prayed she would absorb the message that her identity was wrapped up in God's goodness and love for her. Her parents had definitely dropped the ball when she was a kid.

They'd dropped it in a major way her eighteenth summer. Basil stiffened with anger again at how they'd treated Hailey and pushed her to abort his baby. But he couldn't undo it. Couldn't change the past.

God was perfect in all of His ways. He provided undeniable love, unexplainable peace, because of who He was.

Please, Lord, let that be enough for me. Let that be enough for Hailey. Please lead us through this time into Your light.

Because, while there were promising signs that Hailey was warming to him, she still seemed a frightened animal, ready to retreat for cover once again if he slipped up, even a little.

No pressure.

A buzzing sound came from the floor at their feet, and Hailey lurched forward to grab her purse. The sound increased as she got her hands on her phone and turned off the sound.

Relief radiated from her body at the silence.

Basil wanted to snicker, because who hadn't had their phone ring during church? No one in this millennium, that's who.

But then she gasped and stiffened again, and he glanced at the display. A text from... he couldn't quite make it out.

"I need to go," she whispered and tilted it toward him.

Wesley: I'm taking Kass to Deaconess. She's bleeding.

No way.

But Hailey was already shoving her phone back in her purse and rising to her feet just as Pastor Tomas stepped up to the podium. Had there been more songs? Basil hadn't noticed, but no way was Hailey facing whatever had happened alone.

She edged out of the row, and he followed her.

All eyes were on them now. He could feel them, but he avoided direct eye contact with anyone, even his mom and dad. Even Nonna. Hailey was everything that mattered, and what mattered to her was her cousin. So, Kass mattered to Basil, too.

He tried to catch up to Hailey in the foyer, but she put on an extra burst of speed. Pretty impressive jogging effort in three-inch heels. "Hailey, wait. Let me take you."

"Did you drive to church?" The church doors swung shut behind them, and Hailey paused to peel off her shoes.

"No, but it will only take a min—"

"My car's closer."

She was right. He grabbed her hand, and they both broke into a jog toward the alley behind the bakery. "Has she been okay until now?" *Dumb question, Basil.* But whatever. He needed to keep Hailey's attention on the here and now.

"She's been tired. Taken a lot of time off."

"I'm sorry."

"Me, too."

"Do you want to run upstairs and change?" She looked great in that turquoise dress, but who knew how long they'd be at the hospital? The waiting rooms got chilly and uncomfortable if you had to hang around long.

She shook her head.

"I think you should. They might not know what's going on for a little while, and you'll be more comfortable."

Hailey stopped in the middle of the sidewalk and pulled her hand from his. "Comfortable? I don't deserve to be comfortable." Her voice rose. "Kass could be losing her baby, and the least I can do is be uncomfortable with her."

Basil took a deep breath and grabbed her hands again. "Honey, it's not your fault. There's nothing your discomfort can change. Or atone for."

Tears sprang to her eyes. "You can't know that."

"I do know that." He tried to radiate as much compassion as he could, with or without words. "Take two minutes. You probably need to run upstairs for your car keys, anyway."

Hailey fished in her purse and came up with a keyring. "I do not."

He snatched it from her hand. "I'll start the car and get the AC going. It's pretty warm for September. You run up and change."

"I hate you."

The words pierced his heart. She didn't mean it, did she? She was feeling cornered. Trapped. "We'll talk about that later. For now, you're wasting time when you could be changing." He pulled her back to a jog. "Jeans, not shorts. Grab a hoodie or something, too."

"You'll freeze in what you're wearing."

Good. She'd accepted he was coming. "At least I'm in long pants. If I get cold later, I'll run home and get a hoodie, but I'm willing to bet I won't get you back out of there until Kass is okay."

"You got that right." She burst into a full sprint.

The woman could run in bare feet. Hopefully she wouldn't stub her toe on anything, 'cause that was gonna hurt. She slowed as they entered the alley then tapped the code on the backdoor before blasting through. She was halfway up the stairs before the heavy door latched behind her.

Basil unlocked her car, settled into the driver's seat, and turned on the ignition. Hot air blasted from the vents, but it would cool quickly. She kept a tidy car, which shouldn't surprise him.

It only took a minute for her to reappear and jump in the car. "Hurry."

Good thing he was driving, not her. "I'm not breaking the speed limit. Plus, I'm not running any traffic lights or stop signs." Been there; done that; got the ticket. To say nothing of jail time and the rest of the mess.

She made a rolling motion with her hands.

"Seat belt."

Hailey growled as she snapped the buckle.

He slid the car in gear, put the pedal to the metal, and arrived at Deaconess Hospital in record time. Hailey poised with her fingers clutching the handle as he hit the brakes in front of the ER.

"I'll be inside as soon as I park. Text me if you need me."

She nodded and dashed from the car.

Basil took a deep breath and drove out to the main parking area. It took him a couple of minutes to find a spot and lock up Hailey's car.

Wow, this morning wasn't going anything like he'd expected. Did this mean Kass was losing her baby? Because that was going to hit Hailey really hard, and he'd been nowhere in sight twelve years ago when she needed him. This time — yeah, it was different, but he was going to be right there beside her, supporting her, showing her his love.

"Lord? Please reveal Yourself to Hailey as her good, good Father."

The hospital doors swished open in front of him.

21

*L*ow voices came from inside the cubicle when Hailey skidded to a stop beside Aunt Lenore and Uncle Farrell. She hugged her aunt and spoke quietly. "Is Kass okay? Is the baby okay?"

Then her gaze focused on her parents just beyond. Oh. But how much did she care what they overheard?

Aunt Lenore hugged her back. "I don't know. It doesn't look good."

"Is Wesley in there with her?"

Her aunt nodded.

Mom stepped closer. "Often, if there's a miscarriage, it means the fetus wasn't developing properly. This is probably a blessing in disguise."

Hailey stared at her mother. "Seriously?"

"They can always have another." Mom lowered her voice. "A bit more distance between children is also for the best. Eleanor is still so young."

"That fetus is a human life. It's not a convenience or an inconvenience. It's a *person*."

"It's not a person until it's born, Hailey. You know that."

"I do *not* know that. The psalmist says God formed his innermost being, shaped his delicate inside and his intricate outside and wove them all together in his mother's womb. That's not a blob at all."

Mom shook her head and exchanged a glance with Dad. "I think scientists are quite clear as to when life begins."

Hailey pushed her hair away from her eyes with a trembling hand. Was her mother purposefully trying to rile her up? Because it was working. A red sheen slid over her vision. "So, I was nothing to you until after birth? No connection before that at all?"

"Now you're putting words in my mouth, hon—"

"And still no connection to this day."

"Hailey Ann." Dad cleared his throat. "Don't speak to your mother that way."

"What way? Because it's perfectly clear to me. You guys never wanted a child at all. You remained disengaged from me in utero, and that never changed."

Dad looked around as though wondering who was overhearing. Which was a laugh, since he knew almost no one in Spokane. Besides his brother, who stood right beside him. "Hailey."

Her mother sighed. "It's easier if you don't get too emotional."

"That's what you call love? A bit over-emotional?" No wonder Hailey was so messed up. No wonder she didn't know what love was.

"Sometimes disengagement is the only way to cope. You of all people should understand what I'm trying to say."

Hailey leaned in close to her mother's face. "Don't you even go there."

"Why? You did nothing wrong. I mean, the timing could have been better, but we solved the problem."

"My baby was not the problem. *You* were the problem."

A rattle and a gasp came from beside her, and Hailey became aware that the curtain to Kass's cubicle had just been pulled aside as the doctor brushed past. Kass stared at her. Wesley stared at her. Her aunt's hand rested on Hailey's forearm. Lenore was likely staring at her, too.

No! Her mother had trapped her into revealing everything. Okay, not everything. Not yet, but the rest was coming any second.

Sobs gutting her, Hailey whirled away and slammed straight into a solid wall. The wall had hands that caught her waist. "Hailey."

And Basil had overheard. Sure, she'd already told him, but this was worse. This was public. This was her cousin — her best friend — in her own time of grief and need. Kass shouldn't have to put up with Hailey's mess stealing the show. Kass shouldn't ever know that Hailey had killed her own baby.

"Easy," whispered Basil as his arms folded around her. "Easy does it."

For a moment she melted against him, but no. She wasn't letting him in, remember? She pushed hard against his chest, and his hands fell away. She sprinted past the chairs in the waiting area and out the sliding doors.

Why had she come? Why had she thought she could hold it all together if Kass was losing her baby? Like their experiences had anything in common!

Hailey found a quiet corner behind a sign and folded over herself, trying to hold in her own loss like she had done for twelve years.

Mom had fed her those lies back then. *An unfortunate mistake. Just a blob of tissue. We can make everything right.* Why had she listened?

Because she'd spent the summer flinging her beliefs by the wayside like candy tossed from a fire truck in a parade. She'd had plenty of practice ignoring the still, small voice inside her for a couple of months before she and Mom had had this heart-to-heart. It finally seemed like she could do something right where her parents were concerned.

What kind of messed-up thinking had that been? The kind where a little girl — yes, eighteen, but still so young — had craved her own parents' love... and never received it. Not Mom. Not Dad. Not ever.

No wonder she struggled to see God as a good Father. She had no idea what that was. Her dad had checked out, physically and emotionally. Uncle Farrell was marginally better. His eyes had been opened when Aunt Lenore left him for several months. She'd insisted on counseling before returning to him, and he'd reluctantly given in. While their marriage hadn't been wholly healed, it sounded like things had improved quite a lot, from what Kass had told Hailey.

But Uncle Farrell hadn't been much of a daddy to Kass, any more than his brother had been a good dad to Hailey. Hailey's grandmother had tried to make up for it in the years she'd lived with them, but Grandpa mostly remained busy and aloof.

What was a good father, anyway? A man who loved his child. Who provided for her. Listened to her. Hung out with her. Encouraged her. Corrected her with compassion instead of condemning her.

Dad was such a failure.

But God. He was a Father to the fatherless... which

Hailey might as well be, for all the good having parents had done her. She'd held herself together. Rebuilt her grandparents' business. Pretended she was A-OK.

She was not even a tiny bit okay.

Sobs rent her body and escaped.

Oh, Lord, what had she done? She'd killed an innocent child. Basil's child. And now everyone knew what a monster she was.

To be fair, her parents had always known, but now her aunt and uncle knew. Wesley and Kass knew. The shock and horror on Kass's face told the story. Worst of all, Hailey had announced it herself at the time of her cousin's greatest need.

Hailey gave way to grief. For her own baby. For the lies and the coverups and the false front she'd presented. For the fracturing it now represented in her most precious relationships.

But God. Did He offer pardon after all this time? Real, true forgiveness? If He didn't, who did?

࿇

BASIL REACHED for Hailey as she dodged away from him, tears streaking her face.

Edgar stretched his arm in front of Basil. "She needs a moment."

Did she? Basil glanced at Edgar then toward Hailey. The doors swished shut behind her. The leg of her skinny jeans and her sneaker-clad foot was the last he saw of her.

Kass gasped, clutching her stomach. Wesley leaned over her, breaking Basil's line of sight.

What was he doing here? He wasn't anything to Kass.

He'd only met Wesley a few times, and Kass's parents less than that. And he'd only met Edgar and Louise once before this week. He hadn't made the best first impression. Or second.

There wasn't anything he could do here. There might be nothing he could do for Hailey, either, but he owed it to her to try. He brushed past Edgar and headed to the door but stopped cold at Louise's casual words.

"Basil was involved in that unfortunate incident."

He pivoted. All six pairs of eyes were focused on him. Hailey needed him, but her mother had thrown down the gauntlet, and he could not resist the challenge. He had to set the record straight. For the sake of Hailey's reputation. His own was too far gone to matter.

Basil focused on Kass. Whatever spasm she'd undergone seemed to have passed, because her gaze held his. Was that compassion? He could only hope.

"I ran into Hailey in Venice the summer after she graduated from high school. Her parents"— he skewered them with a look —"were too busy to take time for her and left her on her own to explore Italy. I'd never really paid any attention to her here in Bridgeview. She was just my kid sister's friend. But in Venice, I noticed her. We hit all the tourist spots together and..." He hesitated. "And, well, we were together night and day."

Kass swallowed hard. Wesley grasped her hands.

Basil saved all his attention for her, ignoring the other generation most certainly listening in. "We used condoms. Apparently they are not one-hundred-percent effective, but I didn't know Hailey had conceived when I returned home from Italy and she went to spend the last few weeks of her summer vacation with her parents, who finally had time to spend with her."

His blood still boiled at the thought of a pair of self-centered individuals just letting their teenage daughter roam a foreign country for six weeks by herself. "I guess I figured we'd pick up where we left off when she returned to Spokane. But we didn't. She lavished attention on every other guy in the vicinity and gave me the cold shoulder. I was no more mature. I flaunted my poor choices in front of her, and never made a significant effort to reconcile. My choices only became worse and worse, as you all know."

He didn't really need to go into detail, did he? No. This wasn't the Basil Show. He turned to Edgar and Louise. "But when Hailey found out she was expecting, she told you. Her parents. And instead of offering any kind of love and support, you told her to get an abortion. For your own convenience."

Kass gasped, but Basil couldn't face her. Not when he had Louise North pinned, staring back at him from wide eyes. "You had sensitive discussions with the papal office and decided it would look bad if your unwed teenage daughter was pregnant, so this was the easiest way *for you*. Hailey only wanted to please you. Wanted you on her side. So she did it."

"Nooo." Kass covered her face with her hands, and her hunched shoulders trembled. "Why did I never guess something this deep was wrong?"

"She hid it. From everyone. I only found out a few weeks ago. I admit, I was furious with her." He fired a glare at Edgar. "But then God grew some compassion in me. Her parents failed her, but so did I. It wasn't their fault she was pregnant. It was mine."

Aw, man, was that a crack in his voice? So much for getting this story out in a logical progression. A guy wasn't supposed to get all emotional.

Where had he heard that, anyway? Not from his dad, that was for sure. Raimondo Santoro lived life large but also with his emotions hanging out all over, and so did his brothers.

Basil took a deep, shuddering breath. "That was my baby. My child. And I never even knew. Never had the chance to know him or her."

"You were just a kid yourself," Edgar said gruffly. "Would you have married her?"

"I would have." Basil managed a choked laugh. "And we'd probably have been divorced in a year or two. We weren't ready. You're right about that part, but the choice was taken from me."

"Until you've been a father, you can't possibly understand how hard it is to let a daughter go."

Basil stared at Edgar for a long moment. "But you took that chance for fatherhood from me. Tell me how you supported Hailey. What do you mean, let her go?"

The man glanced at his wife, who closed her eyes and swayed.

What was all that about? Basil couldn't begin to guess. He wasn't even sure he wanted to. Not when the woman he loved was out there somewhere crying, and he wasn't present, holding her. His Hailey was stronger than anyone else he knew, but even she had a breaking point, and she'd reached it. His job was to assure her of his love through thick and thin. Forever.

He stepped closer to Edgar, forcing the man's gaze back to meet his. "I love your daughter. I did a lousy job of that when we were kids in Venice, I'll grant you. But God has shown me real love in the past couple of years, and I'm ready now to be a grownup and love Hailey the way she deserves. I want to marry her, with or without your blessing, but I know it would mean a lot to her if you gave it."

Basil stuck out his hand and held the man's gaze. Was Edgar going to shake it or ignore it as he had on the rooftop the other day? But then they hadn't had an audience. Hadn't been in the midst of an emotional family moment.

Edgar gripped Basil's hand. "You've got it. May you do a better job of guarding her heart than I ever did."

"Oh, I intend to, sir. I definitely intend to." Basil swept a look around at the others in the room. Louise clutched her husband's arm, her gaze still shuttered.

Basil didn't have time for that. Not when Hailey needed him.

22

*H*ailey stumbled up the steps at the back of the bakery, pausing at the door to her apartment. She couldn't confront the space she'd shared with Kass, knowing she'd failed her cousin today. Instead, she climbed the last flight of stairs and emerged on the roof.

She stood back from the railing lest anyone catch sight of her, but the warmth of the sunny September afternoon couldn't seep into her chilled body. She might never be warm again. Never be carefree again.

Her phone rang, and she glanced at it. Basil. This was something like the fourth or fifth time he'd called.

She couldn't face him. Couldn't face anyone. She'd have to figure out how by Tuesday morning — she didn't really have the luxury of phoning in sick like Kass had been doing. Reina and Julissa couldn't manage without her. Not with all the standing orders plus all the baking for the display cases out front.

Her life closed in on her. Suffocated her. She'd been

skating along on the surface, but the ice had cracked, and now she was about to drown in dark, freezing water.

A guttural cry came from her inmost being as she huddled inside the hoodie Basil had made her wear.

"Jesus, help me. I've screwed up more ways than I can count, and I just don't want to be here anymore. I don't want to face this monster that's been let out of the cage. I want to run. I want to hide. I want it all to go away."

But that wasn't the answer, was it? She'd spent twelve years hiding, waiting for the other shoe to drop. The time was now. Pandora's box could not be restuffed. Relocked.

"I'm so sorry." She choked on the words. They seemed completely inadequate. She'd said them thousands of times since that summer, but sorry wasn't enough. Sorry wouldn't bring back her baby.

Nothing could.

Jesus forgave. She knew First John 1:9. Now she thumbed on her phone and read it in several translations. The Passion Translation stood out: 'But if we freely admit our sins when his light uncovers them, he will be faithful to forgive us every time. God is just to forgive us our sins because of Christ, and he will continue to cleanse us from all unrighteousness.'

Forgive. Every single time.

Hailey either believed the Bible, or she did not. Either she believed God forgave her when she asked — because of Jesus — or she did not.

Which was it going to be? Wallowing in the pain and torture she'd been enduring, or face what she'd done and let God's forgiveness wash over her? It would feel like the warm, gentle breeze flittering across the rooftop patio, wafting the sweet smell of chrysanthemums over her.

"Jesus, I'm sorry. Please forgive me. Please take away the sting of my sin." Finally naming it out loud loosened the band around her chest slightly. "I've pretended for years that nothing was wrong in my life, that I liked things just the way they were. Lord, I pray you will give me courage..."

Was it her imagination, or had the current of air shifted a little? Because she could have sworn it wafted the pungency of thyme toward her.

Of course. Hailey smiled as another band loosened. God was sending her a little message with that aroma, just like Basil had done with all those bouquets dotting the bistro's tables on Tuesday morning. Courage.

She'd read Psalm thirty-one the other day. She'd lingered on verse twenty-four, which was speaking about the Lord: 'So cheer up! Take courage, all you who love him. Wait for him to break through for you, all who trust in him!'

At the time, the waiting had seemed interminable. Now, today, she could see she only had to reach out and grasp the breakthrough in faith.

"Lord, give me faith. Give me courage. Help me to accept Your forgiveness and to walk out of this in freedom. I can't live like this anymore. I don't want to."

Another scripture popped into her mind. Psalm 18:19, this time: 'His love broke open the way, and he brought me into a beautiful, broad place. He rescued me — because his delight is in me.'

Hailey tipped her face toward the sun and felt the warmth on her skin. *God's delight is in me. This is a beautiful, broad place.*

Her phone rang again. Basil? Not this time. Kass. She tapped to accept the call as she reached for a sprig of thyme. "Hey, Kass..."

"Hailey? Are you okay?"

"I should be asking you that."

Kass's laugh sounded shaky. "You first. Basil... explained... after you left."

Should Hailey be relieved or not? It didn't matter. She'd left him little choice. "I made such a mess of things that summer." She took a deep breath and pressed the thyme between her fingertips. "And the whole time since, I've been pretending that everything was okay when it wasn't. I'm done with that now."

"I'm so sorry, Hailey."

"Yeah. Me, too."

"God forgives. So do I."

"Thanks." Somehow, she managed to get the word past the big lump in her throat. "I don't deserve it, but—"

"But God's amazing like that."

"Yeah. He is."

"You should also know that Basil looked your dad in the eye, told him he was going to marry you, and asked for your dad's blessing."

Hailey choked on something between a laugh and a sob. "Not again."

"Again?" Kass sounded perplexed.

"That was his opening line to Dad when my parents arrived Monday night."

"I take it they brushed him off then? But this time they shook hands."

Hailey scrunched her eyes shut, which somehow scrunched her fingers, too. Thyme filled the air. "Wow."

"Are you going to say yes?"

She let the silence stretch for a few seconds. "Tell me how you're doing, cuz. Is... is the baby okay?"

"No." Kass's voice choked up. "Jesus took him home. Or her."

"I'm sorry."

"Me, too. I suspected things might end this way. I never felt this kind of sick constantly with Eleanor. But I couldn't help hoping and praying everything would be okay."

"Everything I can think of to say sounds pious or dumb. I'm just really, really sorry you guys had to go through this."

"Thanks. Oh... Wesley went to sign me out, but he's back now. We're headed home."

"Are Astrid and Robert with the kids?'

"Yeah."

"Do you want me to come by? Bring some dinner?" Hailey glanced at her watch. Was it even anywhere near mealtime?

"Lenore's got it, but thanks. There's one thing you can do for me, though."

"Anything."

"Hear Basil out. I've suspected for years you guys had a thing for each other, though I never dreamed it went this deep. It sounds like God's really been working in his life in the last few years, though. So... give him a chance?"

"Well, I don't know..." Hailey managed to keep the grin out of her voice. She hoped.

"You said *anything*."

"But I meant to help you. Take Eleanor to the park. Run a load of laundry. That sort of thing."

"Hailey! I have to go. Promise me."

"Talk to you later, cuz." Hailey ended the call and chomped the sprig of thyme. The flavor exploded in her mouth. Where she was going next was going to require all the courage she could muster.

HE SHOULD PROBABLY TURN his key back over to Hailey, but right now, he was thankful he hadn't. He'd driven back across the city, up one street and down the next, keeping a sharp lookout for her, but he hadn't seen her. Either way, he decided to leave her car behind the building where it belonged.

She'd been ignoring his calls, too. One last try. Knocking on her door hadn't brought any attention, but a glance up the stairwell revealed a sliver of light. The top door was ajar. That either meant Hailey was up there, or maybe it had been left open by mistake.

Basil mounted the steps and emerged into the shadow of the mechanical area.

"Talk to you later, cuz." Hailey's voice. And it sounded light.

Hope lifted. "Hailey?"

She screamed and whirled around, searching the shadows as she grabbed a ceramic pot of herbs.

"Hey! It's me." He jogged forward a few steps, holding his hands up to protect his face if she threw the planter. She was taking the courageous symbolism of thyme too far. He held out her car keys. "I was just returning your keys. And checking up on you."

The pot thunked to the patio as she stared at him. "Thanks."

"You okay?" Did he dare assume she'd accept his comfort now when she hadn't at the hospital? He eyed her. Best to wait for her signal.

"Kass's baby didn't make it."

He poked a toe at the nearest table leg. "I know. I'm

sorry."

"They'll be okay, I think."

He nodded. Watched her take a deep breath.

"I will, too. God... you know God forgives, right?"

Basil's heart hammered. "I do know that."

"God rescued me. Forgave me. He wants to bring me into a beautiful, broad place because He delights in me." Her voice sounded full of wonder.

He got it. He'd felt the same when he finally began allowing God's love to seep in.

"Basil... I..." Her fingers tucked her hair behind her ear, and her gaze met his. She'd never seemed dearer to him as she stood there, looking uncertain, biting her bottom lip.

He waited. Why? It seemed he should, but still she hesitated. He glanced at the little jar on the table beside him and grinned as he plucked out the sprig of thyme tucked inside. He held it out to her.

Hailey took a few steps closer, accepted the herb, and crushed it. As the aroma filled the space between them, she met his gaze again. "Basil, I'm sorry. I'm sorry I toyed with you. I'm sorry about... about the abortion. I'm sorry I spent over a decade ignoring you and belittling you and demeaning you. Can we start over?"

He held out both arms, and she stepped into his embrace. He gathered her close. "I don't want to start over," he murmured against her ear.

"But..."

"I'm sorry, too. I've wronged you in as many ways as you've wronged me, probably more. I forgive you. Will you forgive me?"

"I will. Absolutely."

Basil's pulse picked up at her choice of words. "Then

let's forgive each other, but instead of starting over, let's start from right here. We have a history that can't be erased, nor should it."

"You want to tell your parents."

He held her face between his palms and pressed his forehead against hers. "I think we need to."

"Okay."

"Okay?"

"Yeah. You're right. Hiding our — my — sin has only led to a festering abscess. I'm afraid to open it up to the light of day, but I think it's the only way to full healing."

"I think you're right. I'm sorry, sweetheart." She swallowed hard, and he swept his lips over her jaw. "I'll be right beside you, my love. I'm not going anywhere."

"Is that a promise?"

He trailed kisses across her cheek and up to her temple. "You've got that right."

"Basil?"

He paused with his lips on her eyelid. "Yes?"

"Kiss me properly."

"If you insist."

"I do."

Great words. It was his goal to hear them again in a public place with Pastor Tomas presiding, but not today. Today, right now, Basil covered her mouth with his and felt every nerve ending in his entire body come alive.

Maybe they shouldn't put off those *I Dos* for too long.

23

*H*ailey clung to Basil's hand as they walked up the sidewalk to his parents' house. She'd been here hundreds of times as a teen, but always with Jasmine. Never with Basil.

He squeezed her fingers with one hand and rested the other on the doorknob as he looked down at her. "Ready?"

She shook her head. "Not really." Not if the churning in her gut was anything to go by.

Basil pressed his lips to her temple. "We're going in."

"Okay." They'd been over this all afternoon. Prayed together. Basil had called his mom to make sure they were both home and didn't have a houseful. Evan, the perpetual law student who still lived at home, was out with friends.

The door swung open, and Grace stood in the opening, her gaze ping-ponging between them. Her smile widened when she noticed their clasped hands. "Come on in." She turned. "Raimondo, the kids are here!"

Basil's hand shifted to the small of Hailey's back as she

stepped inside. For just a second, she leaned against his touch, gathering strength and courage.

"I've got you," he whispered.

Ray draped his arm over Grace's shoulder, a knowing grin crossing his face. "Hailey! What a pleasant surprise. Come on in, both of you. I must say, I didn't see this coming."

His wife glanced up at him. "You didn't?"

"No. Should I have?"

Grace laughed. "I think so, yes. Come, have a seat. I'll bring a tray of coffee and biscotti, and then we can talk."

Basil led Hailey into the living room and pulled her onto the love seat beside him. She could feel a slight jiggle beneath their fingers entwined on top of his thigh and glanced up at him. "You're nervous," she whispered.

"Am not." He winked at her.

Somehow, it soothed her a little that he was jittery, too.

Ray settled into an easy chair across from them. "How is Kass doing? I understand she was pregnant and lost the baby."

"It was a hard day, but she'll be all right. Wesley is taking good care of her, and her dad and stepmom are here for a couple of more days."

"That's good. Having family nearby when trials hit makes a big difference."

"I'm sure." Hailey offered a small smile. She hadn't experienced that, not like the Santoro clan would have. The only constant in her life had been her cousin.

Grace offered them a tray, and Hailey accepted a mug of coffee. To take a biscotti as well, she'd have had to let go of Basil, and that wasn't in the cards for now. Maybe later.

Then Basil's mom took a seat and looked expectantly between them. "Tell us everything! When's the big day?"

The poor woman had no idea.

Basil squeezed Hailey's hand. "That's not why we're here. I mean, we're not engaged, at least not yet. But we're here to tell you everything."

Grace glanced between them "Okay. Go ahead."

They'd rehearsed this. Basil would tell the first part. Hailey would fill in. He got the basics of their summer fling out then paused.

"Oh, my. We had no idea." Grace looked at Ray.

Ray shook his head. "And that's when the rebellion began."

Basil grimaced. "I'd been floundering before that, as you know, but yes. That summer set my feet on the wrong path. I quit college. Drank too much. Ignored God. And you know where that led me."

"And now?"

Basil glanced at Hailey and covered their clasped hands with his other one. Then he looked back at his parents. "There's more."

"Oh."

This was Hailey's cue. She took a deep breath and sent another prayer heavenward. "I got pregnant." And then she told the rest of the story of that long-ago summer.

Tears filled Grace's eyes long before Hailey was done. When the words stopped, Basil's mother knelt beside Hailey and pulled her into an awkward hug. "Oh, my child. What a hard path you've trod."

Child. Hailey gulped back sobs of her own. "I'm so sorry I terminated."

Grace hugged her tighter. "I'm sorry, too. And yes, we

will mourn. But I meant you. You were only a child yourself and failed by those who should have supported you and loved you regardless."

"I was eighteen. Not a child." Or at least Hailey had felt very grownup.

Ray helped his wife stand then stretched his hands toward Hailey. "Come here."

She stood, and before she had a chance to wonder what would happen next, Basil's father enveloped her in his arms. "Thank you for telling us," he said in a low voice. He opened an arm to Basil, who stepped into the three-fold embrace. "And you, my son."

"Let me in, too," Grace said with a watery laugh as she edged into the group.

"There's a little more to the story," Basil said.

Hailey heard Grace's soft intake.

"Hailey and I have talked things out. We were selfish and immature back then, but God has been working in both of us, and we've forgiven each other. We're working toward a long-term relationship, but we needed you guys to know what was in our past."

"Remember that parable about the foolish man who built his house on the sand?" Ray asked.

"The floods came and washed it away." Hailey remembered.

"But the wise man built his house on the rock. What happened to that structure?"

Basil chuckled. "When the storms came, that house stood strong. And I hear where you're going with this. Because Hailey and I had the weakest of foundations, worse than sand, even. When the storm hit, every flimsy thing we'd built just fell apart."

Hailey looked up at the man beside her. The man she loved far more, far deeper, than ever the youth in Venice. "But we've salvaged some of the planks from that poor weather-beaten framework, and we can rebuild it on a better foundation."

"'Unless the Lord builds the house, those who build it labor in vain,'" quoted Ray.

Grace nodded. "Psalm 127."

"So, yeah." Basil's mouth quirked into a grin, and his eyes warmed as he met Hailey's gaze. "We're asking God to rebuild the mess we made, and I guess we're asking your forgiveness and support and help, all in one."

"Oh, son, you have that. Your mother and I prayed for this day for many years." Ray smiled at Hailey. "We didn't know you would be part of it."

"I didn't, either. But I'm thankful to be here."

Thankful to be forgiven. Thankful to be loved and accepted. Thankful to have found the courage to face the past and put it in its place.

Thankful to be God's beloved child.

∽ ∾

BASIL FOLLOWED Hailey into her apartment a couple of hours later. He shouldn't stick around. He knew that. But he also couldn't quite bring himself to be apart from her. It had been a massively emotional day in so many ways. She needed him. He needed her.

Edgar struggled up from the sofa as they entered. "There you are." He looked between them.

Well, so much for overwhelming temptation. It seemed the day's turmoil wasn't quite over.

Basil rested his hand on the small of Hailey's back. "We had coffee with my mom and dad."

Louise came in from the hallway and leaned against the wall. "We went out to Frank's Diner."

Somehow, Basil struggled to envision this power couple eating in a repurposed railway car, although Frank's was a revered icon in Spokane. "I hope you enjoyed it."

"We did." Louise looked at Edgar then over to Basil and Hailey. "I need to apologize."

Hailey pressed back against Basil, and he slid both arms around her from behind. He'd support her any way he could.

"For what?" Hailey asked at last.

She could be forgiven for the question. The list of her parents' wrongs was lengthy, as far as Basil was concerned. It was amazing she'd turned into such an awesome human being. He had her grandparents to thank for that, no doubt. He had a few vague memories of them from when he was a teen stopping by the bakery for doughnuts, but he hadn't known them well.

"You're right that I never wanted children." Louise looked down, wringing her hands. "I don't know if I ever told you about my own childhood."

"Not much." Hailey's voice held steady. "I know your parents died and you were raised by your aunt."

Louise grimaced. "She didn't want to be saddled with a child. There's nothing worse than being a burden. Being unwanted."

Basil bit his tongue. What did he know of that? His parents had been there for their kids. They might not have been perfect, but he couldn't blame them for his follies.

"I got through by staying out of her way as much as I

could. Not rocking the boat. And, later, by appealing to her common sense when it seemed she might listen."

The beginnings of her diplomatic career, Basil suspected.

"Anyway, I met Edgar in college. Traveling the world in political circles sounded so glamorous. Very opposite the bleakness of my upbringing. So, we married and went off on our adventures."

"And then I came along and ruined everything." Hailey's voice was full of hurt.

"I felt that way at the time." Her mother looked up with tortured eyes. "I'm sorry I didn't appreciate the gift we were given. I was a terrible mother and was so relieved when Edgar's parents agreed to take you in. I knew I would mess up. How could I do better than the way I'd been raised?"

"All I wanted was a mommy and daddy who loved me, like all my friends had."

"I'm sorry."

Edgar cleared his throat. "I'm sorry, too. The solution seemed best at the time, but I can see now that it was shortsighted."

"Dare I say, selfish?" Basil kept his tone conversational.

The man's gaze flicked off Basil's. "You could say that and be accurate. I know it's not enough to be sorry. It doesn't undo anything, but it's all we've got at this point in time."

Hailey's body was stiff within Basil's hold. He could feel the battle inside of her, because he felt it, too. He breathed a prayer, knowing that Hailey's next words would make or break everything between her and her parents. Possibly between her and Basil, because if she refused their olive branch, could he be certain she'd really pardoned him, either?

"God forgives liars and cheaters and abusers and murderers." Hailey's breath came out in a shuddering whimper. "He forgives. That's what He does."

Because He's a good, good Father. Some of his favorite lyrics ran through his mind.

"And if He forgives, I need to do the same." She gently pushed Basil's hands from her waist and stepped out of his embrace.

Her mother met her halfway. The two women fell into each other's arms and clung together, sobbing.

Basil glanced at Edgar, who stood watching with a look of longing on his face, hands clenched at his sides.

This family was such a bunch of amateurs at this hugging business, but Basil had been raised with the best. He clapped a hand on Edgar's shoulder and nudged the man toward his wife and daughter. Then, as Edgar enfolded them, Basil did the same.

This day would be one for the memory books, for sure. Basil didn't know when there had been so many tears of sadness and tears of gladness. So many group hugs.

So much healing.

It had been way overdue.

24

*I*t was hard to trust her staff, even with a promising new worker in the bakery kitchen. Reina had assured Hailey they could handle the entire day without her, even though it was the Saturday after Thanksgiving.

She and Basil had spent Thursday with Kass, Wesley, Sebastian, and Eleanor... and Wesley's ex-in-laws, Astrid and Robert. Astrid had brought a sugar-free pumpkin pie that vied Hailey's traditional pastry in both texture and taste. And Kass had whispered in Hailey's ear that she and Wesley were expecting again. This time, Hailey rejoiced with her cousin.

But, today, Basil had invited her to the Santoro festivities at the community center. The clan was way too big to fit inside anyone's house. Hailey had to laugh, remembering the driving force Basil's dad and uncles had been in renovating the former art gallery into a community center a few years back. They'd managed to get several grants, including one that paid for the solar panels on the roof and the Tesla

Powerwall attached to the reclaimed bricks over by the kitchen door. The commercial kitchen itself was state-of-the-art, and the hub of Kass's monthly cooking club as well as countless community events.

No wonder the Santoro men had been all over the project. Hailey could see that now, with the way this boisterous family nearly filled the place.

Marietta sat in an armchair facing the door, for all the world like royalty awaiting her subjects.

Basil chuckled in Hailey's ear. "Looks like Nonna is the first stop."

"Looks like." Hailey pulled him closer then bent to hug the elderly woman. "Hi, Marietta. You look good today."

"I am well. All my family is together. This makes a good day." Then a cloud seemed to pass over her face.

"I miss Uncle Al, too," Basil murmured as he air-kissed both his grandmother's cheeks. "But I'm glad to see Aunt Winnie happy."

Marietta nodded. "Charlie is a good man. His other daughter came for Thanksgiving. That is good, si?"

"Very good." Hailey straightened and looked around. Evie Jalonen hung out with her sister, who was married to Basil's cousin Dominic. Dominic and Katri had married just a couple of months after his mom and her dad had tied the knot last spring. They were so cute together. Young, but adorable. Well, not that young. Maybe it was just that Hailey was old. Dominic was a full medical doctor, after all, and Katri was a nurse.

Winnie's daughters, Brittany and Gabriella, hung out by the kitchen with Ava, Dafne, and Marley, but the teen boys, Landon and Michael, were nowhere to be seen. They were probably part of the mob playing basketball under the bridge across the street.

Hailey's gaze shifted to the door as Jasmine and Nathan entered, little Lillian on her daddy's arm. Jasmine's face brightened when she saw Hailey. "Hey! I'm not used to seeing you at Santoro events."

Basil jabbed his sister's arm. "Get used to it. Hailey's going to be around a very long time."

Not that he'd made that hint official. Hailey didn't miss Jasmine's quick glance toward her empty ring finger. The time was coming... wasn't it? They'd been in counseling the past couple of months with Pastor Tomas and his wife, Juanita, singly and together. Hailey felt like they'd been growing by leaps and bounds, dealing with the past and moving to the future. They'd even given their testimonies together in front of Bridgeview Bible Church.

Marco and Daria came in, escorting their three sons over to kiss their great-grandmother's cheek. Caden, twelve now, glanced up at his mother. "May we go play basketball *now?*"

She ruffled his hair. "Go for it, but listen for the dinner bell."

"We will." He grabbed Oren's arm and the two of them bolted away, leaving Arie reaching for his little cousin, Lillian.

"Who all's out there?" Basil asked Marco.

"Alex and Evan will herd them all in at dinner time. It's quieter in here without them."

Basil chuckled, a sound that was always music to Hailey's ears. Then he grasped her arm. "Have you met Rob's wife, Bren? They just arrived from Helena." He waved vigorously, and the couple over by the window sauntered over. "Rob, I'm sure you remember Hailey from when we were kids."

"Sure do. Nice to see you again. I've been hearing rumors about you and my cousin here." Rob grinned at her. "This is my wife, Bren. Davy is out playing basketball with Michael and the others. Lila is…" He looked around. "Somewhere with Tieri. They've got Oliver. At least, I hope so."

Bren smiled at Hailey. "Nice to meet you."

"Same to you. I remember hearing all about you when you and Rob were dating. Fran is a good friend of mine and kept me informed."

"Sisters!" exclaimed Rob. "Hard to keep secrets when your sister tells everyone everything."

"And she's working for you now, I hear," Bren went on. "That's great. She and Tad ran back over to the house for a forgotten container of baked goods."

Basil rubbed his belly. "I'm glad they remembered in time." Then his hand caught Hailey's again.

It felt so natural for their fingers to tangle whenever they were near each other. Now Basil tugged her toward Tony and Kenna, who were being shooed out of the kitchen by Grace. Hailey laughed. The aunts were probably kicking Tony out of the kitchen because he wasn't the chef in charge of this turkey dinner… and Kenna out before she burned a pot of water. What an unlikely couple they were, but how they complemented each other in their care of Marietta.

Tony bent and scooped up a little girl.

"Who's that?" Hailey whispered.

"Oh, that's Tony's sister Gina's little girl, Emma. They live in Galena Landing." Basil pointed. "That's Chris, Gina's husband, talking to Marco. And Ethan"— he looked around —"is over there with Arie and Gavin."

"And this must be your other uncle and aunt?"

He nodded. "Come, let me introduce you to Tony's parents. They live in Galena Landing, too, so they don't make it to every Santoro function." He towed Hailey between the tables. "Uncle Matt, Aunt Connie, this is my girlfriend, Hailey North. Hailey, Matt and Connie Santoro."

She would have recognized him as a Santoro anywhere. Basil's generation might be taller and leaner than their fathers, but the genetics ran true all the same. "I'm so pleased to meet you."

"And we, you." Connie leaned in with the typical air-kisses. "Are we welcoming you to the family?"

A flush crept over Hailey's face. "We've only been dating a few months."

Matt laughed and thumped Basil's shoulder. "Don't let a good one get away, boy. When you know, you know."

"Yes, sir." Basil's fingers tightened around hers. "Don't I know it."

At that moment, Ray tapped the microphone in the far corner. "Can I get someone to call the basketball tribe to come wash up, please? And the rest of you, feel free to find your seat. Some of our young ladies have created a seating arrangement with place cards, so you'll have to look for your spot."

"I'll call the athletes," announced Peter. He grabbed Sadie's hand and they headed for the door.

"Don't forget to come back!" yelled Nathan.

Everyone laughed as a grinning Peter pointed his finger at Nathan.

"Where are we supposed to sit?" Hailey looked at the

place cards nearest them. This was apparently the teen boys' table judging by the names on the cards.

"Hmm. Let's look over here." Basil steered her past where his uncle Franco helped Marietta to her feet.

"Oh, that will be the head table for your parents' generation, won't it?" Hailey pulled against his grip.

"Ah, you're right. We're right here, along with Jasmine and Nathan and Peter and Sadie."

Still seemed closer to the front of the room than Hailey would have expected, but whatever. *Someone* had planned the layout, and who was she to complain that they were situated near the tables groaning under their load of turkey and fixings?

It took a surprisingly short amount of time for everyone to find their places and quieten down.

Ray waited at the microphone, then prayed a blessing over the meal and the gathering before announcing which order the tables would get their food. As expected, the older generation went first, Betta and Genevera dishing up a plate for Marietta.

Then it was their table. Hailey wasn't sure how they deserved preferential treatment, but again, who was complaining? Basil nudged her ahead of him along the row of tables. "White meat or dark?"

"Dark, thank you."

He stabbed a couple of pieces and set them on her plate. "Want some dressing? It'll give you courage."

She laughed out loud. "I thought I smelled thyme. Of course. Sign me up. I need all the daring I can get."

He chuckled and plopped a spoonful on her plate then another on his own. They carried on past the potatoes, gravy, and a vast array of vegetables and salads before sitting down to enjoy their meal.

She leaned over to him. "I'm surprised your family has turkey for Thanksgiving. It doesn't seem very Italian."

"We're American. All of us except Nonna. She'd say she's Italian first, but she loves turkey, so there's no argument from her."

"Basil?"

"Hmm?" He turned to her, poised with his fork halfway to his mouth.

"Thank you for inviting me. I've never experienced anything like this before."

"You're welcome." He bobbed his eyebrows and turned back to his food.

All these years of being envious of Jasmine's family, and here she was. It was a lot to take in.

GOOD THING BASIL had a cast-iron stomach, because his nerves were crawling up his esophagus and threatening to disable his tongue. That would be a first.

He sat where he could keep an eye on his dad, who'd long ago finished a large slice of pie with a mountain of whipped cream on top and now sat back, hands crossed over his belly, swapping tales with Kenji Ito.

Basil hadn't even noticed the quiet Japanese man come in. He'd been a friend of his grandfather, whom Basil barely remembered. Nonni had passed away when Basil was just a kid. Kenji and Nonna had resumed a friendship a couple of years ago. For a while, everyone had speculated that there might be a geriatric romance in the making, but it seemed they'd all been wrong. It didn't seem anyone or anything could distract Nonna from her primary task of ruling her entire clan.

Finally, Dad leaned forward and said something to Uncle Dino across the table. Then he nodded at Basil before rising and stepping in front of the microphone again. "Welcome aboard Santoro Airlines flight 2021. This is your captain speaking."

Basil laughed as the entire clan erupted in clapping and whistling. The pilot came out of his father at the most random times.

"Your dad's a hoot," Hailey whispered.

"He tries." Basil's leg jiggled then Hailey's hand rested on his knee. Oops. She was going to wonder why he was so nervous at a family Thanksgiving dinner.

"We've got a wireless microphone here today," Dad went on, lifting it from the stand and showing off its cordless status. "I'm going to pass it around, and I want each of you to tell us one thing you are particularly thankful for this year. I'm going to start over here." He handed the mic to Rob, who was seated at the other end of Basil and Hailey's table.

"Yay, I get the first chance to say how thankful I am for my wife and my family!"

Everyone laughed.

"And I'd like to announce that we'll be having a baby in springtime, a sister for Davy, Lila, and Oliver."

Applause exploded.

Bren took the mic. "Rob stole what I'm thankful for." She handed it to Jasmine.

"Um, I can't top that one," Jasmine said. "I'm thankful

for my brother Basil moving back to Bridgeview and settling down." She winked and handed the mic to Nathan.

"I'm thankful we're not having a baby in spring," Nathan deadpanned. "Lillian needs a little more time before we're ready. But congrats to you guys." He handed the microphone to Basil.

Here went nothing. While Hailey's attention had been on the others, he'd managed to get the little box out of his pocket without an obvious production. Now, microphone in hand, he glanced at the woman he loved.

"This year, I am thankful for many things. I'm thankful that God forgives, and I'm equally thankful that Hailey forgives." He slid off his chair and knelt beside hers. "Hailey Ann North, I'm so in love with you, and I'd like to ask you to make me the happiest man in this room by agreeing to marry me."

She stared at him, her eyes filling with tears as her hand covered her mouth.

"There's a lot of awfully happy men in this room!" called Marco. "We're hard to beat."

There was a ripple of giggles.

Hailey did a little dance in her seat.

"Will you say yes, Hailey? Because my knee is killing me."

Full snorting laughter came next from those around them.

Hailey plucked the microphone from his hand and set it on the table before placing her palms against Basil's cheeks. She leaned close and brushed her lips against his. "Yes," she whispered. "Together at last."

"We heard that!" called Peter. "Congrats, you two!"

As applause grew around them, Basil rose and gathered Hailey to her feet as well, kissing her soundly.

"Think of the children!" yelled Fran. "Don't look now, kids."

Basil smiled against Hailey's mouth. "Just in time. Or should I say, thyme?"

"Cute play on words."

"Thanks for thinking I'm cute." He sank to his chair, pulling her into his lap, and continued kissing her.

Someone tapped the microphone, and a squeal reverberated around the room. "Hard to cap that," Peter said, "so I won't even try. Like Jasmine, I'm thankful Basil came home and jumped right back into Bridgeview Backyards. And I'm so very thankful for my beautiful wife, Sadie. It's our first wedding anniversary today. Way to steal our show, Basil!"

"Any time." Reluctantly, Basil allowed Hailey to slide over to her own chair. She looked so beautiful when she was flushed.

Sadie took the microphone, but Basil wasn't paying attention anymore. "How about New Year's?" he whispered to Hailey. "I don't need a big wedding. Do you?"

"A new year. A new life. I could get on board with that."

"Let's make it happen." But first, they needed to get through the rest of this family dinner.

*T*alk about a double whammy, not that Brittany Santoro hadn't seen this coming.

She managed to fake a thrilled squeal in her cousin's ear. Yay! Ava and Seth were engaged! Seth had been romantic enough to propose on the national day of love. Whoop-whoop for them. Their love had conquered all the crud life had thrown at them, like Seth's discovery of his baby son not long after he'd taken over raising his two orphaned half-sisters.

Brittany was happy for Ava. She was... and she'd be the greatest, most supportive maid-of-honor any bride ever had, but where did that leave her? Besides single and alone.

The second whack to her ego? Basil, the cousin they'd all loved to hate. How bad could being single be, when Basil managed to make it look fun and effortless, at least if you overlooked his drinking problem and his DUI? But he and his long-time secret love, Hailey, had tied the knot just after New Year's.

Brittany might not be the oldest cousin still single —

there was student-eternal Evan, after all — but she might as well be. She hadn't made the same mistakes as Basil, but she'd come close. Whew that her obsession with Duncan hadn't ended in pregnancy. She and Ava had danced for joy in their apartment kitchen the day her period had arrived.

Lessons had been learned — go on the Pill. Hide any evidence.

And find a nicer guy. One with staying power... because Brittany didn't want to wait over a decade to nail down a wedding like Hailey had done.

Britt still couldn't believe Hailey and Basil'd had a thing for each other for a dozen years and no one had guessed. But if they could successfully lead a secret life, so could she.

Still, it was getting old, and she was only twenty-four. Why wasn't Jeff her knight in shining armor? She'd been so sure. But sleeping with a major client of the ad studio she worked for had been a major faux pas, and Janice was extremely disappointed in her young protégée.

How was Brittany going to break it to Ava that she'd been banished to northern Idaho for the next six months to work for Janice's sister, the mayor of Galena Landing? Ava might need another roommate. Hopefully, she wouldn't rethink asking Brittany to be her maid-of-honor. Britt would be home every weekend — she hoped — to help plan that wedding.

Ugh. She'd keep the reasons for her banishment a secret. Brittany was good at those. She'd pretend this venture into small-town life was her own idea. Yeah. No one was going to believe that. She'd made no secret that even Spokane was too small for her. She was aiming for New York.

Well, here was her chance, right? She could refuse Janice's so-called offer, jump the next plane for the Big

Apple, and try her luck. But then the truth would come out — Janice would make sure of that — and no reputable ad agency would hire her.

No. She had to spend the summer in podunk Galena Landing, population five thousand. Get in, design amazing graphics for their small-town farmers market and whatever else the mayor tossed her way, and get back out with a robust portfolio.

Next step, New York.

This was only a minor detour. Watch her.

So, we've come to the end of the twelfth and final Urban Farm Fresh Romance, but you readers have let me know you're not happy to be finished with the residents of Bridgeview! You keep reminding me there are more Santoros who need to find their happily-ever-afters.

I hear you. I do. And you may have heard me whisper that I've crossed series lines before; why not again? I mean, Rob Santoro's story was told in *Other Than a Halo*, the second tale in the Christmas Romance at the Miss Snowflake Pageant series. (Incidentally, though authors probably aren't supposed to have favorites any more than parents are, Rob and Bren's romance is very high on my list.)

The two names you keep mentioning are Dafne and Brittany. Your wishes have been granted.

Brittany's story will kick off the new Farm Fresh Market Romance series set in Galena Landing, Idaho, home of the original Farm Fresh Romances, my best-loved series of all time. You'll also get to hang out with the original crew at Green Acres Farm!

If Treyan Ackerman wants to keep seeing his daughter on weekends, he needs to stay put, keep his nose clean, and not make waves. Thankfully, he has a decent, if somewhat tedious, job in his small town's municipal office. If the mayor would let him tackle some of the graphics for the farmers market, it would help. But, no. Instead, she hires a vivacious city girl who turns Trey's head. Unfortunately.

Brittany Santoro needs to redeem her reputation, rebuild her portfolio, and relocate, preferably to New York, where they'll appreciate her graphics design genius. But if she doesn't want the whole world to know about her indiscretions, she needs to spend six months in podunk Galena Landing, furnishing artwork and ads for the town's farmers market and other tourism marketing. Too bad the brooding, hunky weekend farmer in her office seems immune to her charms.

But when Brittany connects with Trey's hurting daughter and sees the tender side of him, all bets are off. How can these two wounded souls be nudged into the realization that everything they want and need is right here in this wide and pleasant place?

valeriecomer.com/place

You can read all about Dafne in *Kiss Me Like You Mean It, Cowboy*, the fourth Cavanagh Cowboys Romance novel:

Blake Cavanagh is determined not to be like his father, so he'll play the field and never settle down at all. It's a bit daunting stringing along three women at once, but he's up for the task. When Blake sees one of his girlfriends in line at the coffee shop, he sneaks up behind her.

Dafne Santoro — single mom, new teacher, and city girl — has just arrived in small-town Jewel Lake. She's not expecting to be accosted at the Copper Carafe, and her jiu jitsu training kicks in. Oops. She might exchange fervent apologies with the handsome cowboy as she helps him off the floor, but let him make it up to her with a date? Not happening.

Blake's not going to give up so easily, and Dafne's not about to give in. What will it take to get this cowboy and this teacher on the same page?

valeriecomer.com/kissme

Are you subscribed to my email list? This bi-weekly newsletter is the best way to be kept up-to-date on what I'm working on, what's for pre-order, and what sales or promotions might be happening. Plus, you get a free copy of *Promise of Peppermint*, the prequel to the Urban Farm Fresh Romance series, as my thank-you gift.

valeriecomer.com/subscribe

If that's a fuller inbox than you prefer — but you're still interested in occasional news — follow me on Bookbub and/or Amazon to keep up with new releases.

See you soon in Galena Landing!

FARM FRESH MARKET
ROMANCE
BOOK 1
A Wide and Pleasant Place
USA TODAY BESTSELLING AUTHOR
VALERIE COMER

DEAR READER...

Thanks for reading *Together in Thyme*! I'm so honored that you chose to spend the last few hours with Hailey, Basil, and me. You are appreciated.

Even though our era in Bridgeview has ended, we'll be back for occasional visits through Dafne's story (Kiss Me Like You Mean It, Cowboy — winter 2022) and Brittany's story (A Wide and Pleasant Place — spring 2022).

I'm an independent author who relies on my readers to help spread the word about stories you enjoy. Would you take a few minutes to let your friends know? Facebook, Instagram, Goodreads... wherever you hang out online.

Also, each honest review at online retailers means a lot to me and helps other readers know if this is a book they might enjoy. I'd sure appreciate your help getting word out.

I welcome contact from readers. At my website, you can contact me via email, read my blog, and find me on social media. You can also sign up for my newsletter to be notified of new releases, contests, special deals, and more! Click here to subscribe. You'll receive *Promise of Peppermint*, the novella that introduces Bridgeview — Rebekah and Wade's story — absolutely free as my thank you gift!

- Valerie Comer

www.valeriecomer.com

http://valeriecomer.com/subscribe

ABOUT VALERIE COMER

Valerie Comer's life on a small farm in western Canada provides the seed for stories of contemporary Christian romance. Like many of her characters, Valerie grows much of her own food and is active in the local foods movement as well as her church. She only hopes her imaginary friends enjoy their happily-ever-afters as much as she does hers, shared with her husband, adult kids, and adorable granddaughters.

Valerie is a *USA Today* bestselling author and a two-time Word Award winner. She writes engaging characters, strong communities, and deep faith into her green clean romances.

To find out more, visit her website at www.valeriecomer.com, where you can read her blog, explore her many links, and sign up for her email newsletter, where you will find news, giveaways, deals, book recommendations and more. You can also find Valerie blogging with other authors of Christian contemporary romance at Inspy Romance.

www.ingramcontent.com/pod-product-compliance
Lightning Source LLC
Chambersburg PA
CBHW050730180626
46814CB00002B/685